D0975437

DELIRIUM

A NOVEL

ALSO BY DOUGLAS COOPER

AMNESIA

DELIRIUM

A NOVEL

DOUGLAS COOPER

HYPERION

New York

Library of Congress Cataloging-in-Publication Data
Cooper, Douglas, 1960–
    Delirium : a novel / by Douglas Cooper.—1st ed.
        p.   cm.
    ISBN 0-7868-6341-2
    I. Title.
    PR9199.3.C6435D45   1998
    813'.54—dc21   97-28778
                                                                                     CIP

Book design by Peng Olaguera

FIRST EDITION

10   9   8   7   6   5   4   3   2   1

It is not uncommon for great artists to die twice. Personal extinction is followed by public questioning of the real magnitude of the man, leading his survivors as they bury his body to tear his icon from the altar they themselves raised during his lifetime. Thus death comes as a release not only to him but to those who have gradually found his presence as oppressive as it is inescapable. Often as not the image is later restored, by a generation no longer forced to share the world with him, though the effigy they fashion is likely to reflect as much of themselves as of him. Similar modifications continue through time.

—FRANZ SCHULZE, FROM THE PREFACE TO
MIES VAN DER ROHE: A CRITICAL BIOGRAPHY

ACKNOWLEDGMENTS

Delirium *was serialized by Pathfinder on the World Wide Web. I'd like to thank Barry Deck, who designed the Web site and was my partner on various electronic projects, had a powerful influence on the tone of the final work, and was responsible for much of the success of this book in its digital incarnation.*

An excerpt from this novel appeared in Grand Street. *Another section was the basis for an architectural installation at the Milan Triennale, and was published in the catalogue.*

Jesse Sheidlower was kind enough to read and comment on an early draft.

While writing Delirium, *I have collaborated with architects Diller & Scofidio in various other media—video, dance, and laser disc installation—and had I never encountered their uncompromising artistry and lust for the intellectually perverse, I doubt I would have found whatever it took to persevere with this project over six years. I have no idea whether they would endorse the contents of this package, rendered in this archaic medium, but I owe them a great deal as mentors and friends.*

Jennifer Barth, my editor at Hyperion, is the hero of this tale: she worked on the novel right into her ninth month of pregnancy, and gave birth to her daughter the day after the final manuscript was submitted.

Finally, I would like to thank the Ontario Arts Council for a generous Works in Progress grant, without which I would have lost considerable weight during the composition of this book.

CONTENTS

PART ONE: PLAN

I am a whore.

—PHILIP JOHNSON, ARCHITECT

No life bears scrutiny. On a passenger bus, steel the color of olives, bright halo of dust borne from Sinai to the coming miracle of irrigation, green Galilee, Ariel Price decides with regret that he will have to murder his biographer.

Ariel has spent time in the desert with his memories, and it is clear: the truth is not good. A reputation is a careful thing, built over the course of years by gradual accretion like a coral reef, and this biographer will have to die.

The listing bus shivers on a curve. Ariel Price is thrown against the hard flesh of soldiers. Perhaps he should fear them, their skin made dark by the biblical sun, but he will not. Ariel is an old man, yes, but no less masculine than these boys: he has designed buildings that will outlast regimes; he too has been changed by the sun. An erection rises proudly in his wrinkled shorts. He wills it down, but the flesh does not listen.

Ariel did not expect to remain long in the arid peninsula. His intent was to ponder the origins of holy architecture, the tent in the desert, and then to make his way to the Great Pyramid, where he would study and determine with his own fingers how the stones came together faultlessly without mortar. But the harsh light of Sinai confused him and Ariel Price became lost: forty days and forty nights he could not find his way out of Sinai; he never saw the Pyramids. When he emerges at last from the desert, his hair after decades of severe training has turned against itself and returned to nature. His eyes rimmed with red skin raw from staring down the wind have lost their civilization. The soldiers instinctively pull away from him on the bus.

The green hunched vehicle lurches down the serpentine road to the Dead Sea and the air grows ever warmer as they approach the deep place, the lowest place on earth. Ariel stares into a pocket mirror that he has kept with him this long time on the road. My face has changed.

The wet air wraps him like a shroud, bringing a fine balm of perspiration to the surface of the skin. Ariel Price has made a decision, and over the course of forty days this decision has emerged as a physical fact: his body now registers the rejection of life in its very substance. Ariel has been an old man for years, but only now does he look as if he is dying.

The white hair is parching yellow. The square jaw now a frame for sagging flesh: it reads merely as structure, the system of support; his face hangs from this frame like a mask. Only the eyes are alive, but they are wild, shining with delusion, the glitter of madness: *this biographer must die.*

Izzy Darlow has never heard of Ariel Price. He knows better than to disregard a story whose birth is cruel, however: the story that insists upon making itself heard will be heard, and it is always best to listen. Especially now, when Izzy explicitly searches outside of himself for a tale to make sense of his circumstance, when an entire company of lost colleagues waits impatiently for him to find a thread, this story, however alien, might prove charity. However violent its origins. (And the story does present itself with unusual violence, with the ruin of brick and the breaching of private space, but more of that in a moment.)

Perhaps you do not know about Izzy Darlow? Have you never looked into his life? No? Well, Izzy can hardly expect you to stare into his past when he can barely stand the fact of it himself. You may or may not have met him before, in the wealthy, impoverished city that shaped him; perhaps not. No matter. What is over is over.

Of course, what disappears behind us rarely departs.

Izzy Darlow thought to escape when he left Toronto, when he put his family and city into that shadow box that is his personal history; he thought to find his vision filled with something new, but he was thwarted. Every surface a mirror. He sees himself now in the shape of streets, in the tracery of cathedrals, in the scars and stains on his wooden table. Punishment is optical. Everything a pattern, and his hell to read meaning.

Izzy has taken a room in an old six-story tenement, his floor beneath the creaking roof, the wind off the Hudson so strong that the bed moves at night. Around him the buildings are newer but less human, broad anonymous windows. Some mornings he goes out into the street to find a tall crane planted in the midst of traffic, and hanging skewed from a cable like some obscene fruit, a giant printing press. Only when they swing one of these monsters through a waiting window do the buildings about him take on any hint of program or specificity: this is the printing district.

His own story unbearable, and around him torrents of words fall mechanically from great machines. Amid this silent cacophony, he has been laboring to put together another's story: the story of a man whose life, were it written, might make sense of this landscape, and in so doing might make sense of himself.

There are a group of them, exiles mostly, trying to find this story: actors and dancers. They have a small theater. They have no play. There are no playwrights left in this city; the last was murdered some years ago. Soon they shall meet for the first rehearsal, but they have no text.

Izzy's room, whose windows face north, receives light the color of unstained oak.

His tools are carefully arrayed about him. Pads of pale green paper, quadrille-ruled in faint blue and spiral-bound between golden covers. Technical pens in a variety of widths, but crucially a double zero, finer than any ball pen, with which he scratches his tiny notes. Behind him, a wall of books. To his right, over the sill, he can see into the window across the way, a frame undistinguished except that yesterday a printing press was swung through it like a wrecking ball.

Around the corner they have insinuated wires into buildings, eloquent wires, but here they still print books.

Izzy Darlow owns a treatise on labyrinths. Mere blocks from his apartment is the hidden bookstore, accessible only by elevator, and there he found this latest book. A classic text on the planimetry of delirium. From the dawn of human intelligence, the greatest architects—the first architect!—turned their skills to the construction of paths that led explicitly nowhere.

His new city, Manhattan, is laid out in a grid like a symbolist window, and through that window you can see the Minotaur.

With his few chosen tools, on his oaken desk bathed in oaken light, Izzy Darlow fashions the signs of a life. A life not his own. A story. And, like every story and all stories and The Story, this one rises out of actions almost insignificant, human movement through a bleak tract of earth whose only exceptional feature is that it gives birth, again and again, to all of history. His older atlas calls this land Israel, although the story begins in a part of that land now colored, in the way that only maps and minds are colored, with the tint of Egypt.

Stare at these marks on the page: follow them (their path is a labyrinth in the shape of a straight line), and I promise you that they shall open, like a window—a crack in the teapot, a rent in the page—into a landscape pregnant with dust. Stare at these marks, reader, and my story will catch in your throat.

With these silent words, Izzy Darlow leans over his tinted page, preparing to place ciphers and dots in meaningful lines of ink to thwart the grid.

A flash of light, reflecting, illuminates his scalp. The technical pen remains poised over the grid, frightened to enter the labyrinth. Another flash of light. Izzy Darlow places the tip of the pen in his mouth. A segment of line bleeds into the cracks on his sour tongue. Something metallic is swinging ominously outside his window to the right, but Izzy is concentrating upon the page. Metallic, massy and huge.

What precisely should the first words be? They do not come.

The sunlight sparks off a cylinder of greased steel and briefly sends a cryptic projection across Izzy's wall. He frowns, distracted. A shiver of knowledge: formication. The narrator senses, with certainty, the presence of weight swinging from a taut cable inches from his window. Afraid to look, afraid not to, caught between paralysis and act, Izzy Darlow turns his reflective head ever so slowly toward the window at his right shoulder. Slowly. Willing the frame to be empty. Let there be nothing there.

Another flame of light, this one flooding the periphery of his vision: an object, moonlike, is reflecting the sun; an immense swinging object, moments from the pane at his right. Without knowing why—Izzy Darlow is a lapsed Jew—he closes his eyes on tears and offers a brief prayer to the Magdalene: "Intercede,

Great Lady, on behalf of the fallen, for you too were once human, and it is not easy, not easy . . ."

The glass shatters in a web of shards, concentric circles radiating outward from the point of impact; the bricks scream and shear; the drywall tears in paperlike faults from ceiling to wall to floor; and an infernally complex machine—steel cylinders piled like logs and bound on either side by pinioned frames dense with mechanism—comes screeching to rest inches from the narrator's head.

Izzy Darlow attempts to cry out, but terror freezes the squawk in his neck.

He watches unable to move as the press grinds into motion, still attached by a butcher's hook and steel noose to the crane outside his window, grinds into motion dripping grease on his hardwood floor, and a thin scroll of paper wet like excrement is born.

Fighting nausea, Izzy Darlow begins to read:

"No life bears scrutiny . . ."

The manuscript arrived by courier. The package thin, flat, battered manila, padded with plastic bubbles and sealed with translucent amber tape. It had the air of something shoddy yet dangerous, a bomb prepared by amateurs. Ariel removed the stained photocopy with distaste and pressed the bubbles between his long fingers, bursting the firm round pillows in rhythmic irritation as he read the cover letter.

> Dear Mr. Price,
>   I don't expect you to know who I am. Most architectural historians remain blinded, I suppose, by your

cult of personality, but I am fully aware of how deep your learning goes.

What you need to know is this. I have left a distinguished career as a scholar to join the graduate department at the University of McGill, in the School of Architecture. As a student. I shall return to this irony.

Initially I considered devoting my thesis to your early unbuilt work, but various problems led me to abandon that theme soon after beginning my program of study in Montreal. Theoretical problems. We think broadly, here, under the tutelage of the great Bertram Hyphen, and we are not formalists. I have been pondering alchemy, magical texts, political theory. The Good Life, sir. You have perhaps heard of it? I am not concerned with aesthetics. I try to avoid those mendacious categories under which discussions of your work have managed to turn scholars away from the true nature of your project. Yes, I am a rarity amongst architectural historians: I am concerned with personal ethics. The Good Life, Mr. Price, and whether you, the architect, have led it. This is theory, Mr. Price; this too is very much theory. I am ambitious. And while I have not pursued the cowardly path of less scrupulous men, I have labored to produce the beginnings of a critical biography.

I do not seek your authorization. You would deny it, I am sure. No, I will not beg for your approval. I am sending you an early draft of the first chapter merely to offer you the opportunity, if necessary, to clear up any errors in fact.

The voice was irritating, presumptuous; a bird kissed the pane with a dull, neck-breaking thud. Ariel opened the left half of the casement window and shivered in the wet December blast, the pigeon twitching on the sill. He nudged it with a long knotted index finger and winced as it fell to the gravel five floors below.

His apartment in Paris had a view of the panoptical circus, whose interior he had never seen. Although it reminded him formally of his beloved Palatine Chapel in Akron, the city of his youth, Ariel did not care much for circuses, for this category of human activity, for entertainment. Art should be hard. Even when it is joyous it should be hard, cold, ecstasy born of discipline and deprivation. He had no time for circuses.

A panther rumbled in its cage on the gravel yard. A sleek black paw, swallowing light, passed over the tiny corpse like a shadow. Thank you. Ariel closed the window and returned to the cover letter.

> *I am more than satisfied with the course that my research is taking, but would be happy to explore any path you might suggest.*

On that bus to Galilee, Ariel explores in his mind certain avenues the biographer might wish to essay. The short cul-de-sac that ends in a pool of blood. Perhaps the winding road that terminates dramatically in a cliff and a friendly nudge. Or the open highway, so difficult to negotiate with faulty steering, severed brakes, and the madness of adrenaline.

> *I must admit that, like the rest of the world, I once had great admiration for both you and your work. I*

still admire your work. I hope that relations between us, if they must take place, will be civil.

Yours,
Theseus Crouch

The architect again examined the manuscript, reading parts at random. He closed it. The stain from a cup of coffee had been photocopied onto the first page. An outrageous personal affront: the leaking cup permitted to rest on the first chapter of his biography, and that insult duplicated in black and white. The inner curve of the stain a perfect segment of circle; the outer curve bleeding, irregular.

Izzy's manuscript has no mark, but then it is still wet and new.

Dazed briefly, Ariel permitted his mind to wander freely through the physics of that stain: the movement of the seeping coffee, dictated by fluid mechanics, surface tension, the texture and absorbency of the manuscript. Elegant: the contrast between that perfect inner curve and the random outer line. A building and its garden. A star and its gaseous storm. *What in hell am I thinking? This student is digging up the bones of my life.*

With great self-restraint, Ariel made his slow dignified way down five flights of stairs, the manuscript tucked in a slim briefcase. Slow. Dignified. It was as much as he could do to keep from breaking into a panicked run. This is my life. It is not a comic novel. It is my life. Great architects do not scamper down stairs. They descend.

Rue Oberkampf, a cramped and human street, emptied into the glorious vastness of a boulevard. Grand gesture, godlike urban planning. Nobody has the courage to cut great vistas through the city anymore. Now we hear nothing but "the preservation of neighborhoods." Slum worship.

Ariel had liked the sound of "Oberkampf" when he had first rented the apartment. The High War? The Over-War? Of course, the source of the name proved less interesting. Monsieur Oberkampf was a textile baron or something. Some Frenchified German nineteenth-century captain of industry.

As it happened, Ariel Price had a flight to catch, which he had booked some days before. He would not read the manuscript, not now. After dining early on *tartar chevaline*, he would pack his small bag, then take the train to the airport.

As he walked stiffly by the circus, the panther sneezed. A white feather floated between the bars of the cage and rested rippling on the pavement. You're welcome.

The green bus descends toward the Dead Sea.

PARALLEL LIVES

A single encounter at nineteen confirmed the path of his exile. Standing in his father's shop in Akron, cradling a newly carved gargoyle, Ariel Price came to the conviction that would drive him obsessively for the next seventy years.

The stone monster was one of his father's specialties, a lizard, kyphotic, with leering mandarin features and a prehensile tongue, every scale on the body carved with care to mirror the real. The surface had the cool, papery feel of a reptile's actual skin. Ariel was scheduled to learn, on that day, his father's most cherished secret: how to carve the intricate pattern, the ornamental signature that made the material seem something else, deny itself with eloquent lies.

As he held the blasphemous lizard, Ariel felt increasingly dizzy. The pattern was creeping up his own young arms, leprous. A wave of nausea broke against his chest and scales appeared, bilious green, on the back of his hands. The monster hissed. The tongue reached obscenely for his eyes. The son of the stonemason froze, letting his father's statue fall to the tiles, where the hunched beast shattered into elementary substance. Retching, scratching at his arms—the scales, the scales!—Ariel Price emptied the contents of his stomach into the shards.

Theseus Crouch, already at nineteen betraying the layer of fat that would cushion him and keep him warm until boiling from his bones, crept out of the family bungalow to join the thugs. He pulled on his uniform when he was safely out of sight of the neighbors: khaki, sewn with badges. Tonight he would not paint his face.

London was divided into clans of warring youth, and Theseus wanted desperately to belong. His chosen gang was particularly vicious. Despite his intelligence—perhaps because of it—young Theseus too had an evil disposition, and he thought he might be capable of rising in this sphere.

Unfortunately, his designated friends considered him a dupe and a slave: the plump kid who spoke with a silly accent. Where did he think he was from, London, England? To his face they called him "Teasy"; behind his back (although often within earshot), "Feces."

London, Ontario, was a small city, perpetually shamed by invidious comparisons with Toronto, which itself shrank, detumescent, in its proximity to New York. Theseus Crouch came from a city doubly diminished, the chip on his shoulder trembling.

At first, his response to this gnawing suspicion—that he had been born to irrelevance—moved him to revel in his marginal status: I will make my smallness a virtue. But his fellow hooligans, truly small, resented even him. As he was to find out on this evening.

His faction had no collective name but wore the same outfit, long khaki coats thick with logos sewn from hem to collar, and boasted a cruel leader, a younger boy with fine brown hair to his shoulders and pale skin a riot of freckles. Gavin, the son of a prominent restaurateur, had been raised a delinquent from an early age in the back room of his father's establishment, where cards were dealt and deals forged, the unofficial city council. Gavin was only sixteen, but he had easily moved into the acknowledged position at the head of this murky group; even the eldest were terrified of Gavin's unpredictable whims, and the uncanny strength belied by those thin arms.

Theseus arrived, properly cloaked, at the place where they always met, the tiny parking space in front of the milk store. Gavin, as always, sat elevated on a concrete bollard, catlike in his ease, surrounded by silent nervous admirers: lieutenants, odalisques.

"Teasy." Gavin pointed at him, closing an eye. He was being summoned.

"Yeah. Hi. Hey, Gavin. What's up."

"Teasy will show you how it's done." This to a young girl, new to the group; Theseus had never seen her before. She was pretty, with willful defiant eyes; eyes that seemed to mock even Gavin. "He'll show you good."

Theseus blinked. "Uh, what's that, Gavin? You want me to show you what?"

Gavin smiled and leapt gracefully from his concrete throne; the circle parted. He signaled to the girl—follow me—and melted into the darkness like a leopard. Theseus knew to follow.

Nervous laughter behind him, as Theseus trailed Gavin and the new girl to the park. He heard the whispered insult: "Feces ... feces ..." Reddening, hating with the set of his rounded shoulders, he followed.

The park at night fell quickly from the civilizing lamps of the street; they were soon three shadows, indistinct against the trees.

When they had gone a great way down until they were very much alone, Gavin turned. "Christine here wants you to show her how it's done."

Christine said nothing, smirked.

"Don't you, Christine."

"Whatever."

"She does." He was looking at Christine, but he was addressing Theseus, who was now frightened. Gavin opened his army coat and began to loosen his belt.

"I, uh, I don't really know . . ."

"With your mouth, Teasy. Show her. And you'd better watch your teeth; you hurt me, you'll know."

When he had finished, Theseus Crouch knew that he would have to leave London. To leave Ontario. That he would have to erase his life. It was the lesson, irrumation, that would shape his every thought: how the past could contain a moment of shame so deep that an entire future paled in its memory. Theseus Crouch emptied his stomach against a tall maple.

Izzy is concentrating less now on the vile machine teetering on his broken sill than he is on the wet pages in his hand. The stories emerge from the printed text and are mixed by the wind. The map shifts beneath his feet. And one story in particular makes him forget, briefly, that he is cold.

A voice from the stones. A voice no more substantial than the halo that rings the streetlamps on a humid night. You've heard it. Alone at night, walking the downtown streets, you've stood in the steam from a grating and heard this voice. A young girl. There is always crying in the city, and sometimes it's her.

She came to this city to dance. Home was far to the north, but she had been forced to leave that place. When she came down here to the metropolitan area, it was not because she expected to be happy—even the most innocent expect nothing like this from Toronto—but simply to leave behind the shame. Her father had disappeared, and then she had slept with most of the boys in town; it had seemed a fine thing at the time, all that attention, but they began to talk about her, to expect things, and she was made to find another place.

The last night in her town up north, they had taken her, each one of them, in order. Later she would remember the garage in which it happened as if it were not quite real. A dark object. A built shadow. It shone, if that were the word, with negative light, swallowing memories: it became a church for her, a private temple of shame. Always, when she tried to remember home, she would orient herself toward that garage as if in prayer, and her memories would go black like a spreading bruise.

She made her way down with the trucks.

Bethany knew about the truck routes. Her father had driven. The last they heard he was out in the oil fields, working as a swamper, wading through the mud to attach the cables between the truck and the part to be towed. Dangerous work. A rogue cable could cut a man in half. Bethany knew that drivers would pull into truck stops at regular intervals to eat or rest or talk, and she made these her points of encounter. She would fall asleep at a table with a cardboard sign propped beside her: TAKE ME TO TORONTO. PLEASE?

Toronto had seemed to her the most sophisticated, the most dangerous place on earth. The mere shame of a teenage girl from the North was nothing beside the torment and stress of every moment in this city. Here was the great pattern of life. Here she was small.

17

Her last ride was in a pickup truck, which took her down the long street as the sun rose. The gathering together of the city was so fast and terrible coming from nothing: gas stations and roadside patches of settlement angry as weeds giving way to the tall and instantly bleak suburb. The city itself was prefigured by another city, a suburb grown urban, and even this was larger and more wild than anything Bethany had ever seen.

Before he left, her father had taken her on modest excursions, and she would wake after midnight, wrapped in cotton flannel and sleepy, to find strange light caught in the cracks of the windshield: the light of northern cities, Sault Ste. Marie, Thunder Bay; once she had been south as far as Barrie. Even these places were more than her quiet mind could fathom, and she would close her eyes and curl back into the cracked leather seat.

TAKE ME TO TORONTO. PLEASE? It was the question mark that set her apart. In past years the roads had been clogged with dreaming youth, filthy and wide-eyed and far too thin, and the truckers had grown wary. These children did not respect the simple courtesies of the road. There were laws between strangers. For years these had held true, but they were based on the unwritten principle of reciprocity: if you bought a man his dinner as he hitched across the country, it was not so much out of generosity as it was in hope that the same might happen to you should life change. These children understood nothing of this. They were, in every sense, children: they just took, and then took more, and expected that the world would continue to give. By the time Bethany made her way to Toronto, the truckers had grown cynical.

Please? The word itself was rare enough, the pleading question mark almost forgotten: it suggested not simply youth but vulnerability, need made soft by weakness. Though most had given up on traveling children, every man at his coffee still felt a peculiar debt to Bethany. Her kind. Every man had left someone, if not permanently then at least for too long, and leaving puts this accusation in its wake: you have left me, and I may not survive without you. In helping Bethany survive the long journey south, every trucker was paying a small piece of this debt.

Never mind that Izzy Darlow knows nothing about this girl Bethany. Here, too, Izzy has experience: he has seen disparate stories come together as one. Wait. Do not judge. Nor does he try to think too much about how it is that the text arrives. Where it comes from. How it is delivered, and from what place. These things are mysteries. This new story is not enough to keep him warm for long; he is cold again; he pulls on a coat and paces, miserable. The wind blows vengefully through the hole in his ruined wall.

Bethany had no idea where she would stay, or what she would do. The first day she spent wandering between the tallness of the buildings, taking it all in. There were objects made by man that dwarfed even trees; of course she had known this, but to see it, to be made small herself by these creations, was new and struck her with sickness and awe. The first night she had been taken to a shelter for children.

Bethany had decided on the way down that she would give her first name, but not her last, because there was always the possibility that they would try to send her back. She could not go back.

Of all the boys who had mounted her in succession in that

dark garage, only one was as thin and pale as she was, and Bethany knew that he hated himself for being among them. For months she had kept herself from him, sneering, until this night. She had watched his eyes grow painful with obsession like the shadows in winter, and she knew that he had entered her on that night with something deeper and more violent than love: it was retribution, because she had made him feel insignificant, nothing. She could not go back for two reasons. There was the group, and the snickering hatred that bound them against her; and there was this boy, David, whom she now remembered with growing regret. Bethany had given herself to him in a way that would cast them apart forever. She had never wanted him, but now she was both his and not his in a way that made her terribly sad, and she knew that he suffered even more.

Before her father had left, Bethany had never slept with any boy. His presence prevented it, banished the very idea of it: the act was neither permissible nor necessary. But she was thirteen when he left, and a new wilderness had grown within her, the soul once childish and orderly gone tortuous like the map of a strange continent. She needed more and darker things than the world could now give. Bethany discovered that she could want conflicting objects at the same time: comfort and humiliation, closeness and distance, silence and crying. More than once she had found herself naked with boys from the town whose ordinary selves had been wrenched out of shape by the contradictory nature of her desires, her loathing, her need. She brought out the vulgar side of sweet boys, made the brutal ones cry, and both grew to despise her way of making them over into cripples and demons.

She found nothing, of course, in her feverish promiscuity, but further distance from a father far away.

Bethany hoped that the city might harden her in a way that

abuse never did: she had become increasingly weak, and open, and trusting, with every boy who pushed his fingers up her to make her cry with pain. She forgave them every excess because they were boys, and not her father. Sometimes it occurred to her that she wanted one boy, just one, to cause her the pain that her father had caused by leaving, but nobody could, and sexual humiliation was better in her mind than some of the other possibilities: she had considered cutting herself, or starving herself, or lying naked in the snow until her skin went as blue as the air and her flesh froze beneath it.

But no, she had simply taken them all, in barns and garages and adolescent bedrooms, and tried not to hear when they talked about her between themselves: one boy had insisted upon having her when she was bleeding, and had spread the word that she was disgusting, repulsive, a kind of disease. Perhaps Toronto would harden her against this. She wanted to be tough, like the whores who came up from the Sault. Drunk and icy. A little bit dead.

On Yonge Street, later, she met an entire community of these, some of them younger than she was, and it occurred to her instantly that she had been wrong. She did not want to become hard. She wanted to become so weak that the world would tear its eyes out and weep blood for her pain; so kind and soft that every vicious boy would expire with grief; so lovely in her weakness that David would be transformed into a man and would forgive himself, and her, and would take her to Edmonton to meet with her father so that she could touch his forehead and forgive him too.

She had no idea how this could be done. Had anybody ever been this weak, in the history of frail humankind?

The beds in the hostel were pushed together to fit as many as possible into the room, with no space to walk between them. Bethany had never spent a night with this many girls. It was different, somehow, from her night with all of the boys in the garage: strangely, she felt shy around all of these women in a way that she never did with boys. They spoke differently, and had customs learned on the streets of the city that made her feel nervous and tongue-tied. Were they really this arch and dismissive? Did nothing matter to them? Bethany remained silent, and listened, and when it came time to go to bed she made her way nervously down the row of beds and crawled over the foot of the one assigned to her. The lights were still on. She felt exposed, and pulled the sheet over her head. Her eyes were open in this tent of white, so that when the girl next to her reached over to put her hand on Bethany's shoulder, she could see the shadow approaching.

"Hey."

Bethany emerged carefully from beneath the sheet to find an older girl, perhaps eighteen, eyeing her with curiosity. The girl was thinner even than Bethany, with tight black-red curls and thick glasses.

"First night?"

Bethany nodded.

"Where you from?"

"Oh . . . north . . ."

The corner of the girl's mouth lifted, soft irony. Her eyes so deep that Bethany could not tell the pupil from the iris. "That's pretty fucking specific, isn't it. Whole country's north of here."

Bethany shrugged.

"S'okay. You're clever. I don't meet a whole lot of clever

girls here. You don't want to let anyone know where you're from; I bet you left for a reason. I bet you wouldn't be too happy if they sent you back. Once I told them I was from Vancouver, to see if they would send me there: always wanted to see the West."

Bethany smiled. "My name's Bethany."

"Sarah." The girl offered her thin hand, a parcel of bones. Bethany took it, but did not press. She had never met a girl who spoke as carefully and well as this strange, emaciated neighbor, and she was overawed.

"So, um, where you from, Sarah?"

Sarah flashed surprisingly lovely teeth. "Testing me. Clever girl. I just told you: that's not yours to know."

Izzy Darlow in his fractured room on Charlton Street, Ariel Price in the train en route to the airport: both read an excerpt from the manuscript of Theseus Crouch:

> *My search takes me to strange places. Who would have thought this, that the clue to tall buildings resides in the stories told by lost souls, late at night, on the bitter winter streets, in the hostels and soup kitchens and holding tanks. In the places through which men and women move who have never known architecture except as the given, what is simply there, shaping their environment (often, and by design, against their will). These people have something to say.*
>
> *When I despaired of libraries and archives, I took to the streets, and moved among them.*
>
> *The forgotten period—as it came to mind, in my*

wandering, the period that I like to call anamnesis— was gradually revealed to me, in a way that required patience and skill to decipher. I learned a medieval technique to pierce the allegory. For that was the shape in which this information came to me, always. Allegory.

The mind in despair works like the legs of a cockroach, unknowing, on the level of narrative and symbol, in an effort to find a path back. I received what I had to know wrapped in strange cloth, wound about with the trappings of fiction. But as I unraveled the package, unwound the layers of pain, I found nestled at the core, shining darkly, the piece of the story that was missing.

The builder Price, though it would shock him to know this, figures prominently in the mythology of the dispossessed . . .

At night conversation takes invisible wings. The darkness of the hour, the crisp sound of the voice in the midst of silence: these call messengers down. The solitary air denies itself. In the vast and empty quiet, listening begins. A night of such conversation, especially when combined with the terrible loneliness of youth, the urgent need that attaches to all things, one night can forge strong bonds of friendship with almost pathological haste. By the time the sun rose, Sarah and Bethany would be friends, and though they would never see each other again, they would remain friends until the day, not so distant, that one of them died.

On this night, Bethany heard for the first time a story that would alter the course of her self. She was told, in pious detail and with great inaccuracy, the story of a woman who seemed to offer hope to even them, the whore who became mysterious and holy even among the saints: Sarah told her, as she had heard it whispered on the streets of Toronto, the story of Mary Magdalene.

In a terrible place, in a time long ago, there was a woman of great beauty who would lift her dress for pieces of silver. You too will do this, now that you're here, and it will change you. Of all the women through all the ages who have rented the space between their legs, she alone was changed for the better. Let me tell you about this person.

She sits in a window. The windows are not fashioned from glass in this place, but from thin sheets of salt. Harvested from the sea. The storms come, and the sea gives up her salt, and the men collect the flat sheets from the sand and cut them to fit their walls. In that place it is said that a child crying can dissolve a home.

The woman is gazing through a flat crystal. Follow me back through the moments that lead up to this. Immediately before turning to the window, she has been staring into a mirror. She has been applying lipstick. In that time, the lipstick was fashioned from red clay. Before painting her lips, she was lying on the low daybed, her legs pulled roughly to either side by a soldier, his sweat falling into her mouth.

But now she is sitting by a window. Are you following me?

Bethany would follow this voice wherever it led, a voice like a thread of silver.

Sitting by a window. If we follow the story in the other direction, down through time, we find hundreds of painters forcing themselves to the very limits of their talent in an effort to reconstruct this moment. To capture her look.

It is important. It is one of the very great moments in the human play. The precise instant in which she first sees him. She is naked, and she is staring out the window, her lips deep red. The moment of sight is the space of recognition, the fulcrum of change: there is no going back. From this precise point she ceases to lead an ordinary human life. She enters the great room. The chamber of history.

Only now does Bethany understand that this voice too has changed. Bethany's eyes are closed, and the story is carrying her in waves, but the voice is no longer the voice of a young woman—perhaps it never was—but a sound without physical origin, certainly without sex, a voice without species, universal and transcendent. Bethany reaches out to touch the hand of the girl beside her, and the hand she touches is cold. She does not open her eyes.

Of history. We think of change as subtle, and long, but some forms are immediate: rape can change the mind in a white second, violence the body in an instant, conversion the shape of history. What the painters have tried to capture is the moment of conversion. A woman glances out the window, through a sheet of solid tears, and sees a man.

In the better paintings you can see this: how her face has become different. Yes, she was a woman of great beauty, but that beauty was nothing, an arrangement of human features in a pleasing but ephemeral manner, whereas now it is a sign of who she is and will be forever, even into death: the shape of her soul. Because she has seen this man.

The words do not seem to come to Izzy in any specific order, but then they rarely do. The mind is where narrative comes together, and Izzy Darlow never expects his mind to progress in a linear fashion. Let farmers plow the earth in straight lines; I was born to deviate. He receives the many stories as if they were one. This room is too cold for concentration; Izzy Darlow shivers in his coat, his bladder full and uncomfortable.

PARALLEL LIVES

Ariel, as the contents of his stomach mixed with the shards of his father's stone beast, resolved to devote his life to the unmaking of his father's project. He would erase the stonemason's hand. There would be no signature: no gesture, no ornament, nothing but the clean intersection of materials that spoke truth. Ariel Price was a subtle man: he knew that horror need not be pictorial, that even the most simple structure, properly planned and detailed, could appall. He would have no need of gargoyles. Terror, after all, is abstract.

It was at this moment, retching, his father's work in broken fragments at his feet, that Ariel Price decided that he would be an architect.

Theseus Crouch leaned against the soiled maple, his heart making hard noises in his soft chest, his mind a gyre of shame. He could no longer be what he was. He could no longer live where he lived, and he would have to change, make himself over completely, destroy the memory of what he had once been.

White and sick, Theseus recognized that he

could never thrive at the margins. He was a man of intellect. If he were to make proper use of his talents—his intelligence and cruelty—it would have to be in a more subtle realm. Theseus Crouch decided, the reek of vomit at his feet, to go to university. The decision welled up within him: he would become a great scholar; he would destroy whole schools of thought. Once again he leaned forward and retched piteously.

When Ariel's plane touched shuddering down on the runway, white crystals came to steam beneath the tires. Snow was falling in the Mediterranean city for the first time in forty years. His shoes left precise marks in the dust of snow as he stepped across the tarmac. Ariel shivered. The palm trees shivered. In Paris he had been subject to a complete skin search and rectal examination and his face was still sour with the memory. And now this upon landing, snow in Tel Aviv: he wrestled with the incongruity of events.

Tel Aviv itself a paradox. Here was a model city, a city that took up and exemplified modern theory in the face of serious national superstition, yet it left him uneasy. Surely there was nothing about the land itself, the materiality of the tarmac, to engender nostalgic thoughts. The mere fact of arrival in the Holy Land by jet plane could not itself cause a thoroughly modern man to resent theories of planning that had moved him, sometimes to tears, throughout his professional life. And yet.

The way in which the city received his taxi as he sped in from the airport. This was disturbing. Despite himself, Ariel Price wanted some obstacle to present itself: a medieval tangle of streets, a patch of tortured pavement to challenge the effort-less hum of tires, but there was none. A perfect freeway lined with palms and lit from above welcomed his car into the dense metropolis. Flakes of snow moved in confused patterns, some-times suspended still, sometimes rising as much as falling in the artificial light, filling the air.

The cabdriver turned and flashed a gold tooth, winking: "My friend, you have brought a rare gift from Paris: snow for the city of Tel Aviv."

Ariel Price looked away in disdain. The gesture was clear: he had not labored to build an international reputation only to have informal relations with ethnic cabdrivers. The driver's smile froze briefly and the motive visibly drained out. It unfroze. The lip descended like a curtain extinguishing the bright gold tooth. He turned away.

The muscles at the back of his jaw drew tense—Ariel could see them, and thought of the jaw, the inefficient jaw, the worst kind of lever, with the force and the load on the same side of the fulcrum—as the driver focused on the road with fierce, almost religious intensity. After a long stretch, the driver began to mouth alien words. They came at first silently, and then with audible breath behind them, and then with a soft pentatonic melody.

"Excuse me, what are you singing?" asked Ariel Price in irritation. "I don't understand Hebrew."

"It is not Hebrew," said the driver, without turning around. "It is Aramaic. A prayer for the dead."

"I don't see any dead people here."

The driver reached into the glove compartment, whose door flopped open on a single hinge, and fumbled about with his hand. Ariel Price was briefly apprehensive. He leaned for-ward. This was a nation of guns. The driver removed a dusty object, which he passed over his shoulder without removing his eyes from the road.

A cracked pocket mirror.

He turned around again and smiled, so broadly this time that Ariel could see the saliva glistening on his pink gums.

If Bethany were to open her eyes—she does not—she would see her new friend, Sarah, lying cold and blue on the bed beside her, unbreathing, and a young boy perched at the foot of the bed, curled into himself like a monkey, speaking in a neutral voice. Blood on his forehead.

Bethany does not open her eyes. But when she retells the story to a friend, much later, a drop of blood appears above her left eyebrow; she wipes it away, unknowing, thinking it perspiration.

This is the story of how a woman changes. How she becomes beautiful. So that even her bones, in death, are invested with the power to heal, so that men and women will covet them and break off pieces and set them in silver, ordinary bones, kissing them as if they were lovers and hoping that their world, too, will dissolve like a pane of salt into vision.

She is more than one person, this woman. The first is named Mary, an ordinary prostitute. After she glances through the window and is altered, she becomes Saintes-Maries, because there are soon two and then three of her: the fallen woman, the contemplative woman, and the saint. It is a time when all single things, changed, become three.

And everybody who's ever changed or wanted to change prays to her.

All such stories start in the middle, but the middle is not all that you need to know. What you want to know, now that you're here, is the beginning. How does a woman come to that window? Give so much of what matters away? Rent her womb to the enemy, take in his seed and hold it warm in her deepest place as if it were her child, his and a thousand brutal faceless others'?

Ruin everything?

Bethany, her eyes tightly shut, listened to the neutral voice as it found its way from the foot of Sarah's bed into the night between them. Later she would remember this as a conversation, even though she said nothing. Even though, in truth, Sarah also said nothing. The moon, crippled by hungry cloud, filling the cracks and the dust on the windows with reflected light. A web of white veins. And the boy at the end of the bed milky and insubstantial, a refutation of time, death in life, eloquent.

I will not tell you yet who this boy is. He is the storyteller, and he is always here; I will let him announce himself, when the time is right.

Sarah and Bethany communing in silent conversation, the boy began the story from the beginning:

Once upon a time, in a city by the sea, a girl found herself alone. That sea is unlike any other, for the fishermen become heroes, and the fish are named after saints, and crystals of salt as deep as icebergs float mostly submerged, fall into each other with the music of shattering glass, boom, crack, sing as they separate into sheets and wash up sharp and useful on the shore.

Her father was dead.

Saintes-Maries had been told that her father was a fisherman turned hero, one of the great, humble men who would find himself immortalized in the name of a fish, or perhaps in the sign on a church, and she contented herself with her loneliness because it seemed a small price to pay for her father's transformation. Saintes-Maries was a Jew—we forget this now—which meant that her life was woven through with expectation. At any moment the world might shear like a crystal of salt and reveal the miraculous, despite the ordinary, despite the pain that was everywhere.

At the edge of the city, close and yet shunned, were the lepers. Every human body strives to become either a needle or a sphere, and the lepers were the bodies determined to become spherical: the arms would pull into the shoulders, the legs into the abdomen, the features on the face melt into sores. Saintes-Maries lived her life in expectation of the miraculous, but more common—daily, in fact—was the sudden announcement of another form of transformation, harrowing, dire, the scales that signaled the death of beauty.

Disease lived in the water and the food, danced invisible on household air, took you when you were young and faultless and left you vile.

Saintes-Maries, however, strived to become a needle. Through her example disease would cease to have dominion. A lancet. Loneliness was a small price to pay. Someday a part of the landscape would bear the name of her father.

Nor did she fear the demonic. For equally prevalent, and

equally sudden, was the onset of possession; a good citizen might return from the market to his contented family, unaware that hidden between the loaves of bread was a bony traveler, three-fingered and snake-faced, the creature that feeds on sanity, drinks the soul. This man would be perhaps in the midst of spreading the day's provisions on the table for his kind wife, when from his eyes a scent of death would turn the milk, and a thousand voices never heard in that house before would scream from his belly, dividing reason into mutilated pieces, howling down the family like a generation of dissent. At that moment everything good would depart. From here on only misery, poverty; the family name a curse. And it was sudden.

Forty days in the desert has given birth to a decision. Ariel has spent the time in Dahab, in Dar es Salaam, in mountainous places without names. He came down from the mountains with a carefully worded message that he faxed pseudonymously from a small Egyptian town to Montreal. It was a bold message, cryptic and full of noble lies, threatening and wheedling and sometimes even seductive. The fax was received with a period of respectful silence during which Ariel was convinced that he had succeeded in shaking the biographer from his trail. But the answer came soon enough.

> *Dear Sir,*
>
> *I thank you for your contribution to my research, but I must insist that your sources are sorely misinformed. I have checked your assertions regarding Mr. Price, and I regret to conclude that the truth in each case is considerably more tawdry and vile than your*

fax would have it. It is interesting to encounter a scholar with similar preoccupations, but it seems abundantly clear that you have neither the intellectual resources nor the profound moral probity required to pursue an investigation of this order. Never mind. You won't last.

You see, my dear sir: you, like me, will soon be disenamored of your subject. You will discover that, in the choice between perfection of the man and perfection of the work, Mr. Ariel Price has concentrated solely, and to a grievous fault, on the latter. And as I say, it is clear that you do not have the tenacity and depth to continue in this depressing venture once fully informed of the abyss to the edge of which you have blindly stumbled. I would happily send you the first chapter of my critical biography if it might aid you in deciding to leave this difficult area of research to those more qualified.

Yours,
Theseus Crouch

Pity Ariel Price. The circling around of thought, vulturelike, the naked vicious past: once refuse, now carrion, now blood, a moment's wetness in the desiccated landscape. Ariel Price descends in a green bus. He chews a long fingernail. The air grows warm.

Izzy leaves his broken apartment and climbs down six flights of stairs to the street. The crane is standing in front of his door; men are yelling; he avoids them. Upstairs, the press is still spitting wet paper into his room. I just want to be alone, for a moment.

Izzy retires to the diner beside the bank, where the coffee is thin and the waitresses resentful. Izzy Darlow does not belong here. The other customers exchange banter with the staff in strange, cheerful accents, but Izzy has nothing to say. They give each other looks when he enters. Always he leaves a large tip, but this simply serves to augment their disdain.

Today another customer sits beyond the sphere of camaraderie. Her face a web of scars, she is otherwise young and pretty, her mouth smeared with black lipstick. Izzy smiles at her and she turns away, pained. He has pushed a sheaf of damp papers into his pocket; ignoring her, he spreads it on the table, flattens it with his palm, and chooses a passage:

A demon leaving the body was greasy, sated, belly round and tight from eating great pieces of the soul. Saintes-Maries had witnessed this; most girls had; demons were a fact of life, as ordinary as miracles and leprosy. There were men capable of driving the demons out, but they were rare. It took a tremendous effort to confront the parasite; most men did not have the strength even to look into another man's eyes. To cast out demons was a selfless, piteous business, and required the most terrible human contact: one man gazing without flinching into the crawling soul of another. Saintes-Maries had seen it done. It left both men exhausted, like lovers, and the audience reeling with nausea.

Whole cities, too, were sometimes overcome and had to be purged by fire.

Travelers mattered a great deal in that time. There were laws between strangers. For years these had held true, and had kept men from murdering each other in the desert. A visitor was sacred. Sometimes, however, a city would forget its God and begin to pray to something else, something snake-faced and hungry that spoke more urgently to the needs of men, and the laws concerning hospitality would be renounced. At these times, a visitor to the city was not a sacred guest, but the other, mere flesh, a being to be used. Men would hold down visiting women so that their friends might enter them; children were treated as whores and fine men made to do the work of slaves. The human body is flesh when the laws have melted away.

Two cities in particular had turned. They now worshiped smooth creatures with scales, eyes heavy and vulgar, who basked on the altar craving children. Offerings were made live to these new gods. A traveler would do better to starve in the desert, drink urine and die beneath the hammer sun, than test the hospitality of these cities.

It was said that three angels were sent to find out whether indeed these places were beyond redemption.

The angels came dressed in rags. One had the face of a leper. One was crippled. The third, their servant, carried provisions. They arrived at the gate of the first city, and cried for alms.

"Please, sir, I am sick and require food."

The gatekeeper kicked the leper. "Then don't bring your sickness here. This is a clean place, whore."

The angel fell to the dust, weeping, and the gatekeeper smiled. "But your friend still has a face." He took the crippled angel by the back of the neck as if she were a dog and forced her into his shack, which stood beside the barred gate. The shack was temporary, culled from pieces of torn papyrus, many of which had fragments of the laws written upon them, but the man was illiterate. Calling his friends, he invited them to witness as he forced his hand inside the angel, tearing her.

The crippled angel called out in anguish: "Please, you're hurting me . . ."

The gatekeeper laughed, and held up his hand, which was wet with blood. He held her so that a friend could spread her legs and impregnate her. The angel cried, "I am an innocent traveler."

A third friend opened his robe, and the angel wept, "Will no one help me?"

No one stepped forward. The third friend prepared to urinate on the sobbing woman, and the shack was loud with laughter.

Nobody saw the leper and the servant. They were standing, now, at the door to the shack, and they were as tall as cedars.

The crippled angel turned her head to look directly into the eyes of the man standing over her. He screamed. His hand, holding his member, had become a searing flame, and all the lungs filled with the black smoke of flesh. Horrified, the mob started for the door, but standing there, as tall as great towers, were two livid angels, one white and burning with sickness, the other black. All who set eyes upon them clutched their faces in agony, eyes become salt and pouring through their fingers. The gatekeeper, who knew that his shack was papyrus, ran to the back wall, hoping to tear a great passage and escape. But a voice held him, inches from his destination: "Stay!"

And suddenly the gatekeeper could read.

Held there, by a force he could not understand, the gatekeeper was made to read the torn laws that were his home: the laws concerning mercy, and friendship, and hospitality. It was as if he had been sliced in two by a fine blade for all to see: he read and knew that his heart was leprous, his spine crawling with hatred, his stomach a cauldron. As the laws made their way into his being, the gatekeeper grew transparent: if any of his friends still had eyes, they might have seen the inner workings of his body, the soul sectioned and open to be known.

And as the three angels grew, so that the sky was darkened with their height, the gatekeeper and his blind friends wept. Salt poured from their eyes. The sky blotted out, water-borne salt in torrents drenched their clothes. The gatekeeper now a window, and his friends too drowning in salt, the laws blistered. The city grew white with gathering crystals. A great wind came from the east, and in it could be heard a Voice, but no one could make out what it said, and with the wind came a storm of particles out of the desert, white particles, and the city was buried in a hill of crystalline dust. For centuries nothing would grow on the white dune, and if you put the earth to your lips it tasted of bitter work.

The second fallen city lies beneath a lake. It was built by a great tentmaker, a man of intellect. He had made the first temple, it was said: a tent in the desert. Later in history, his friend the Vulture would look back at this simple tent and find in it the origins of everything that mattered, but the tentmaker was never satisfied with his early achievement.

Weekly he walked the road between Jerusalem and Damascus, a straight road, paved with a black substance that glittered if you looked at it in a certain way. The tentmaker had clients in both cities, and he made the trip often, a long walk, and he would think along the way. The road, as I say, was straight, but even the most impeccably linear path conceals detours and forking choices. Sometimes invisible. He walked this labyrinth, a maze in the shape of a straight line, and sometimes he would think on the tents he had made, the ones that housed a Voice and a people, and he would be inexplicably appalled.

The tentmaker had ambitions: instead of a Voice, he aspired to serve a physical presence, herpetic and lazy, and to build for this god a permanent place of worship. Once, in the course of his straight journey, he was struck down by a bolt of electricity from the sky—witnesses said it looked uncannily like a forked tongue extending from the snake-faced sun—and while writhing on the ground he renounced everything he had ever made and known.

That night he took his tentmaker's needle and with it sewed a foreskin of papyrus onto his circumcised penis. And as the blood stained the writing paper and he fought unconsciousness, he conceived in his mind a new city, horribly tall: a towerlike city, a needle to pierce the sack of heaven. And the next day, stooped in pain, the hunched tentmaker began to build the most ambitious structure ever made, an effort—unknown to him—to rival the tallness of the angels who had ruined the first city.

In this new place, a snake-faced god was fed with the heads of saints. Young women danced. The tentmaker was made a potentate, and he would choose virgins from the field to satisfy his increasingly morbid desires. He did not even recognize in himself the deviation of his needs: the road for the tentmaker was always straight, its forks hidden from sight.

One day he instructed his minions to fetch him a leper, a cripple, and a black woman. These would be his evening's entertainment.

In Dahab, Ariel Price paddled about on a rubber raft. A Bedouin had rented him a leaky diver's mask and every once in a while he would put his head beneath the surface of the water to encounter the Other World.

The glorious blueness of the underworld. Ariel had always known this; his entire generation had known this; it was a fact of the mind inherited from boy poets in the nineteenth century: revelation was found below. The unlit water of the underground spring, the yawning spaces beneath the earth, the blue world that opened beneath the blind surface of the sea. These were the places of encounter. Not the rarefied air of mountains, clear, sun-bright, the glowing air of the Mediterranean, no: back to the cave. The cosmos has been inverted, and we go under, now.

Off the shore of Dahab there was a world of midnight cities. Millions of tiny citizens had banded together and died clinging to make hard reefs, with caves and towers and passages to guide the gliding forms of fish the shape of needles and pliers. Ariel would duck his head beneath the surface and find there an argument: a justification for the Dark City, the Sub-City, a life of torment and creation.

We were the first to will our nightmares, not our dreams, into concrete reality. A tremendously courageous decision, this: a pure decision, high and lonely and noble. Only the bourgeois still builds on his dreams.

He remembered the strong nightmare. The one that returned through nights of adolescent fever, building itself higher in his sleeping mind until whole cities were there, cities of solitude, dark ecstasy. Ariel Price was gifted even then with space, with the rare ability to create a complex prism of ether and turn it in his mind, four invisible dimensions. He would dream this growing city ever taller until one night it was so unspeakably tall that the tower at his left and the tower at his right threatened almost to touch at the highest reaches, the sky between them diminished to a single bleak star which they held between their pinnacles, monstrous pincers, the whole sky made small and held in a claw of steel. And every window dark. Every window except one, the tallest window, bright and distant with the lonely light of the mind. Ariel Price knew that he would have to build that city, that entire city, before he could occupy this: the highest, most lonely window.

And there off the shore of Dahab, nature itself had given her imprimatur: my city is correct. Ah, but a photocopied manuscript in a slim briefcase on the hard floor of a Bedouin tent put such conviction to the most severe test. Damn this man Crouch.

The tentmaker occupied an office on the highest level. He knew that in the deeper reaches where the populace worshiped there were writhing deities to appease, but his quarters were high above the labyrinth sunk beneath the tower, and he had forgotten all about the gods for whom he had built this tall city.

The tentmaker had become famous, now, for the burning of tents. He would send his minions into the desert to find primitive temples—often inspired directly by his own early efforts—and would have them torched, together with the worshipers and the Voice within.

It is characteristic of makers who take an invisible turn in the road that they revile the path behind them, all the more for having walked it.

The tentmaker did not reckon with a simple fact of his apostasy, however: Voices do not burn.

"Bring me a leper, a cripple and a black woman. I am bored."

In a miserable tenement on Charlton Street, in the city of New York, Izzy Darlow thinks on the laws concerning hospitality: Am I hospitable? Would I be condemned for what I offer and want from my fellowman?

That night, a tent is burned on the plain. From this tent had been heard a particularly loud and authoritative Voice, and the tentmaker's troops had trembled as they set fire to the walls. Screaming was heard from within. And despite the efficiency of the consuming fire, three women managed to emerge from the opening in the tent, unscathed. One had an injured foot, so that she limped piteously. Another's face was ravaged by the wasting illness, her features melting into a mask. The third was black, a girl from Egypt, beautiful and stern. The soldiers took them back to the city.

The three were led to the tentmaker.

The tentmaker, Ariel Price, sits in his office at the top of a great tower, awaiting his soldiers, who have found for him a cripple, a leper, and a black woman. The tentmaker, who has built not only this tower but the vast labyrinth beneath, waits. He does not know that these women have brought down whole cities before, that they know secret places in his own city that even he cannot imagine, that they are not his.

The women, cloaked, lips smeared with charcoal, are led before the great architect, who looks them up and down approvingly. The eyes from beneath the cloak evaluate him as well, but he is not privy to their judgment.

"Dance for me."

The cripple removes her cloak; beneath it she is draped in rags, and they are insufficient to conceal her misshapen foot. It is hardly a limb; resting against the stone floor it looks like the horribly severed ham of some beast; her foot is bleeding from the forced march. "I'm sorry. I can't dance. You see—"

"Yes, I see. You are crippled. I know. I expressly requested a cripple. Dance."

This last syllable, uttered with the overweening contempt proper only to the makers of cities, cannot be ignored. It cannot be disobeyed. It is a word of tyranny: an absolute law, without hope for appeal; a command.

Shuffling, clearly in excruciating pain, the hurt angel dances.

Ariel Price puts his fingertips together, pleased. He turns to the leper. "And you. You will now take off your clothes."

We know that the woman Saintes-Maries was unhappy. That she found out, too young, that her father who had disappeared was not a hero, but instead one of those fathers who disappears: that she had been left alone.

We shall pass over the destruction of the second city; it is predictable and unnecessary; all we need know is that the city of Gomorrah was drowned at the bottom of a saline lake, a lake so heavy with salt that nothing will ever grow there, and that poets have said that she lies there still, preserved in her criminal state: the tall city now deep.

By the time we come to Saintes-Maries, the city has been long cast down, and is only a memory preserved, a story told to children to remind them of what will happen should they forget the law.

These stories sometimes serve their purpose. Sometimes, however, they go horribly wrong. Saintes-Maries had been raised with this cautionary tale, how the Cities of the Plain had been punished, but once she found herself alone and unhappy, and fatherless, she decided in her battered heart to extract the wrong lesson from that tale, to see whether she too could bring upon herself a judgment so dramatic that her demise would become part of the fabric of communal memory.

And so she began to sleep with soldiers.

Ariel took a taxi up through the Sinai Peninsula, winding between dry red mountains and the glittering Gulf of Aqaba. Travelers were forced to walk across the border at Eilat through a kind of no-man's-land, a blighted strip of buffer territory punctuated by officious men with guns. A ragtag line of pierced and opiated adolescents stumbled behind Ariel like converts, past the tiny huts where lazy Egyptian bureaucrats fanned themselves and slapped at flies and eyed the crazed architect with legitimate distrust. At the border Ariel submitted to a skin search and rectal examination with stoic disdain.

The green bus took him up through the Negev: scraggly farms, undisguised military installations, another desert without sand. A few of the addled children from Sinai are making the trip to Tzvat and view the aging architect with awed respect, wondering at the drugs that have produced such eyes, and the impressive fact that he alone was searched at the Israeli border. The soldiers are made nervous by something more sinister and ancient: Ariel's uncanny resemblance to a figure who had emerged from Sinai centuries before, speaking ominous words, upsetting the civic order, a man whose severed head still speaks in icons and dreams and prophecies come true. The prophet undone by a dancing girl.

In the terminology of that time, we could say that Saintes-Maries began to have her first problem with demons.

The demon that seized her was specific to the young: the urge to give over everything to need, to stop at nothing in the embrace of want, to ruin everything through wanting. What Saintes-Maries wanted was love, but what she opened herself up to was a procession of men, the men who were always moving through town and being replaced in the tides of violence: soldiers. This was the want that is never satisfied, because it mistakes its object: she wanted love, but pursued something else, and the sole outcome was despair.

Imagine a young architect who desires only to sleep with boys, but instead finds himself dressing in the long coats of torturers and soldiers; it is much the same thing. But more innocent.

Saintes-Maries was fourteen. She was donning makeup, dancing for men who prodded her with weapons and laughed, then entered her when she was finished.

Soon the need changed. One too many times she was thrown out into the street when they were done with her, and found herself hungry and fighting with the dogs for diseased meat, and Saintes-Maries decided—or, if you will, the demon decided for her—that she would no longer be free in her slavery. If they wanted her to dance, to mock her and spread her legs when they pleased, then they would have to pay for it.

Now when she found herself in the street after a night with the soldiers, her pockets were heavy with their money. They were forced to treat her with grudging respect; they no longer lay in bed contemptuously as she made her way out the slaves' entrance; they walked her to the door and offered a stiff good-bye. Because now she was rich with their money.

This cannot be taken for respect between equals. It is a balance in the soul, between hatred and desire, made complex by the transfer of money. Men always pay the prostitute twice: once with the gesture that leaves them limp and weak, and once again with the money stolen from their own pockets, stolen from their wives. Twice in a given encounter Saintes-Maries reduced the soldier, until he was forced to acknowledge her. When they left, they were often more unhappy than she was.

It was a dance between losers, the dance of humiliation: as they clung together they drew further and further apart, each wondering silently who had fallen further, who most deserved contempt.

Saintes-Maries became expert in this subtle dance, and famous in the cities of the night. She was greatly loved and greatly hated, admired as she lay naked for them, naked and serene, moments away from violence.

Sarah, or whoever was speaking, remained silent for a long period. Bethany did not mind. She opened her eyes and took in the room around her, the children in their beds, breathing slightly out of sync, sniffling and sometimes making tiny incoherent cries as their sleep took them through difficult passages. It was astonishing what sleep could do to hardened flesh: all of these dangerous children, angry with sharp jewelry and tattoos, and when they slept they reverted to their age. Bethany would have liked to know them, now, in this state, even though she sensed there were few she would want to know in the morning.

Sarah, on the other hand, was a friend. Bethany could not put her finger on what it was about this older girl lying beside her and holding her hand that she was beginning to love, but it had something to do with the ability to make sense of the mess. Sarah seemed gifted with the rare ability to string the vicious turns of daily horror into a story, coherent and meaningful and almost musical in its structure, in the way that things were established and then returned to, changed, so that they reflected a different aspect of life, the way a lens subtly turned will become the window to something completely new. Sarah had been given a story, and as it worked its way through her it became something still old but new with the unique sensibility of an adolescent ruined by the streets of Toronto. Bethany heard the story the way she would examine a diagram of the soul; each secret chapter fell into place and illuminated a dark corner of her own mystery; each way in which the Magdalene changed to meet the incomprehensible made clear to Bethany the way she herself would change in the face of great suffering.

And she was to suffer greatly.

One day Saintes-Maries sat in the window, naked. Her consort had just left, and she was reapplying her makeup, which had become smudged in the encounter. In her hand a tiny pocket mirror, which reflected both her face and the framed view out the window in which she sat.

As she put the red to her lips, that window reflected in her mirror in turn framed the figure of a man.

He was riding by. Beneath him a sad, wise animal: a donkey with knowing eyes. And his own eyes, meeting hers in that unreal space of reflection, were unlike any eyes that have ever seen the world, that the world has ever seen.

The encounter in the mirror between Saintes-Maries and this man changed everything. She could not go back. Her life, ordinary and small, had been changed: she wanted something now that she had never hoped to imagine, that she had never dared want to exist. And there was no return. A meeting of eyes, and she could never again be what she was.

All that matters in the course of human life is meeting. Every moment that matters can be looked at in this way. The first meeting is foundational, but every encounter looks back to this first meeting; every time that we turn away from ourselves to acknowledge the other is a new coming together, and an antidote to despair.

The man was not beautiful. He was too thin, and his eyes too large. But those eyes contained within them such peace and such sadness that Saintes-Maries never wanted anything else again except to know what those eyes meant, what that man was thinking; she wanted to know this so desperately that she was willing to follow him, to drop the pieces of her life and follow him in rags until she had figured out the mystery of being sad and peaceful at the same time.

One moment's reflection in the mirror, and Saintes-Maries knew this: she would have to change everything and follow this man. He had put a question mark in her soul. She turned to look upon him directly, through the pane of salt. This moment becomes paint.

Her first impulse was shame. She put her nails to her face, for a moment she thought that what she had to do was tear into the skin, destroy her beautiful face and with it everything that she had become, but she could see in the man's eyes that this was not what he wanted.

Saintes-Maries began to weep. She emerged hysterical from the house and threw herself in front of the man's animal, crying: "Ride. Ride over me. Let me be the road. I hate myself."

But the man sitting on the donkey made no attempt to do this. The donkey looked at her with compassion, and did not move. The man smiled. He leaned down from the bare back of the animal and put out his hand.

Saintes-Maries did not know what to do. She could not imagine touching this hand.

"Take my hand."

And Saintes-Maries felt from that moment on that she never stopped crying. The tears never showed, but her face did shine as if it were wet, and that is what she felt: that her life from then on was never without tears. There was so much to weep for, and Saintes-Maries knew that she would never finish crying for the world unless she began immediately and never stopped.

Sarah stared up at the ceiling. "Ever notice how the air comes apart when it's dark out? Turns into, I don't know, bits of black sand or something?"

Bethany looked into the darkness around her, and saw what Sarah was speaking about: particles of darkness, which bred and commingled to produce new images at the edge of sight.

"You know, we think we see things pretty clearly, but we don't. Our eyes are fucked. You can tell at night, because everything comes apart; but it's also true in the day: we can't see for shit."

"Follow me." That's all the man ever asked of Saintes-Maries. Or of anyone. "Follow me." Of course, it was not easy. It was perhaps the hardest thing in the world, to follow this man.

You could not just walk behind him. Even the animals that carried him were changed. When he finally got down off the back of his donkey to walk in the streets with his bare feet, the donkey had a mark on its back for life. Not just for life, but for all time: every donkey ever born was now born with this mark on its back, because that was how hard this man was to carry, and that was how much it meant.

And for Saintes-Maries it was even harder, because she mattered to this man in a different way.

He had come just for her. Just for people like her.

Bethany examined Sarah's face as the older girl stared at the wall. Sarah was trying to decide what she thought about this: the possibility that people like her might be worth something. That she was worth something.

"I mean, it's not my fault, is it, that I didn't have this guy stroll into my life, on a donkey. Right? Not a whole lot I can do about that. And so, okay, maybe I've done too many drugs, and maybe I'm not in great shape to sit at some guy's feet and learn—I don't remember a whole lot—but the fact is, he's not here. Right? So it's not exactly my fault."

Sarah did not seem precisely to believe this, but Bethany could not be certain. The face, linked as it is almost mechanically to the soul, undergoes waves of minute and precise transformation in accordance with its master, and Sarah's face wrestled perceptibly with this problem. Was it her fault? Perhaps. Perhaps she might have been better prepared for that man to arrive. But the fact remained: he had not come. He was a figure in a story, removed by centuries and strange clothing, and he had not presented himself to her.

Saintes-Maries sat with this man and his friends, in caves outside the great city, and listened.

What is it keeps a girl there, listening? By now, Saintes-Maries was established in her practice: she could have any man that she wanted, at any time, and she could always walk away.

What kept her?

Viewed from the exterior, it was hardly a life. They sat in a cave. They ate bread. Some knew how to fish, but that is not a life. It was not about comfort. He did not pay them. Saintes-Maries and the other men went from poverty to something even less than poverty, viewed from any perspective other than within.

That, however, is not the way to view them.

Eyes are of no consequence here. Of no use. Light illuminates the skin, and eyes apprehend the surface of things. As Bethany listened to Sarah, she was transported inside, the view of the knife, which slices through the optical, the material, the flesh, to reveal the workings of the ghost, the circulation of the spirit, the precise path whereby the soul makes its way through the labyrinth. Viewed from this perspective, fishermen can become heroes, and Saintes-Maries and her father redeemed.

The section through the bone of the protagonist reveals something more than marrow: it illuminates the quality of desire, what it is that makes this woman and her starving friends lean toward this man the way the heavy head of a sunflower turns toward the sun. Partly it is symmetry: these followers, although lesser in every way, see part of themselves in him, and they look to him as a mirror. Mostly, however, it is aspiration: they want to be what he has told them he expects of them. Most men look at Saintes-Maries and see, at most, an hour's pleasure—an hour against her slick skin on a heaving bed—but he looks into her and sees the rest of time. He sees eternity. What she could mean down through history, until the brass trumpet sounds and time comes to a halt. He breathes meaning into her, and she aspires.

"He sees that piece of her that has nothing to do with this business of being a girl who spreads her legs for men, and eats bread, and shits like the rest of us, but the bit that really matters: the piece of her that the world's best painters will want to paint, and the world's best people will want to pray to, because this piece of her—the piece the guy sees—is so good, so good . . ."

Sarah was crying.

"And what, what really gets me . . .

"What really gets me is that, without this guy looking at her, she could have been anyone. You, me, anyone. She's the one who gets seen. Not us. He looks at her, and sees that she's good, and her life gets turned around forever. Until that brass trumpet wakes up the mountains, and all the bodies that have ever died press their knuckles into their eyes and stretch and get up out of the grave and walk to Jerusalem, and she's going to be there, waiting and content. Because he looked at her. And I'm going to wait here and service greasy men in Toronto until I catch something ugly and no one wants me any more, and no one's ever going to look at me. I've been waiting. I've been waiting all this time and . . . and I'm pretty sure of it. I'm not going to get seen. If I have that part of me that matters, nobody's ever going to see it, and I'm just going to die lonely like everyone else.

"It's not fair."

I will follow you. This is the secret that permits even the greatest torment to seem reasonable, almost bearable: I am following you. Saintes-Maries follows, and becomes prominent in a community of men who will die—as she will—the most painful death of the body, death that maps onto the death of the man who leads them.

They will present him with parts of their body as tokens of their loyalty. I give you my skin. I give you my blood. And, from Saintes-Maries: I give you my eyes.

I will follow you.

Together they enter the great city of Jerusalem, the metropolis to the south. When Saintes-Maries was very young she had driven with her father, who was a truck driver, down from Galilee along the roads that led to Jerusalem, and sometimes she would wake after midnight, wrapped in cotton flannel and sleepy, to find strange light caught in the cracks of the windshield: the light of cities north of Jerusalem, white stone. But she had never entered the gates of the great city itself, and she does so now in a line of filthy men, following a man on a donkey, and the crowd rises to its feet in praise.

Bethany stared into the particles whirling about her, watching them dance and collide, forming shadows beside her bed, and thought about death and what it would mean to turn it inside out. And the grains of night came together, fighting to make something and then failing, as she squinted and tried to think with the part of her body between her heart and her head. At first she could see nothing much, except for shapes that wanted to exist but were not yet ready, but after a few minutes of serious concentration—Sarah's voice faded now to a soft breath at the periphery of her mind—Bethany could see a concrete shape, solid, forming from the insubstantial pieces of the night. Soon the shape ceased to mix with the darkness around it, and stood out clearly: it was a young boy with a gash across his forehead, and he was standing beside her bed.

The girl beside Bethany was silent now, but the story continued. Sarah did not in fact know how the story ended, and it would hardly matter if she did: she was asleep.

Bethany clutched the other girl's hand and stared into the whirling particles of night. Breathing in time to the sleeping children around her, she heard the rest of the tale in the voice of a young boy.

A painting grows dark in a gallery thousands of miles away. In ancient dress, no longer colorful, a whore sits by a window holding a small mirror. Her eyes meet the eyes of a man. The painting tries, but fails, to capture this instant of meeting and the change contained therein: how the man sees infinitely into the darkening woman, rending her before making her whole. Dust on the surface.

The Sea comes into view, a steaming gray expanse breathing salt into the air. A mist of condensation mingles with the dust on the surface of the window and the landscape is refracted through a filthy lens of tears.

Ariel emerges from the bus into the sickly humidity and stumbles along the shore of the ailing water until, nauseated from the journey, he sits heavily on a sharp rock. A voice intrudes carefully into his psyche. At first he believes it to be the mind playing aural tricks, the inner voice of memory, the song of the driver sounding solid and external in that noisome atmosphere, but then it becomes increasingly clear that the voice is female and ancient and real, or at least as real as anything that can be seen by those startling eyes, and that this, the Prayer for the Dead, is being sung by a withered woman in skimpy stained rags—a kind of makeshift bikini—a desiccated hag on a bleak rock some meters out into the sea. Her gray hair is untied and impossibly long, washing about her like seaweed, and her sunken flesh hangs from her bones like extraneous matter and her voice is terrible. *Ysgadal, v'yskadash . . .*

For reasons he cannot begin to explain Ariel Price is moved to strip to his filthy boxers and wade out into the tepid sea.

He is uncannily buoyant in this water. The salt pushes up against his body like tiny hands. He leans back and floats on the surface as if it were a skin against his own. As always, the wonders of fluid mechanics send him off into a fond reverie: he ponders the beauty and mystery of surface tension, feeling increasingly happy with the world, until sharp teeth nip at his ankle and he awakens to his situation: he has drifted far out into the middle of the sea; the rock and the hag have disappeared; he does not know how to swim.

Ariel panics momentarily, kicks at the little monster that is chewing his heel. It rears out of the water, a white skull appended to ribs and a spine, then disappears beneath the salt surface. Ariel Price wills himself to remain calm. One cannot sink in such water. He can feel this. The water is holding him up whether he wishes it or not. Calm.

The song turns over and over in his mind and he is tempted to put his head beneath the surface. Ariel Price finds cities in deep places: Is there a city here? Has nature put a city here, a city of night and submersion, that justifies my own, that makes my dark city good?

He turns, lolling, briefly spasmodic, so that he is facedown, holding his breath. He opens his eyes into the deep salt. They sting, Christ—it is like staring into red-hot steel, abacination—but still he wills them open and open they remain. They see.

Oh yes, there is a city here. A vast city. Steaming, putrescent, preserved at the moment of decay, a sprawling city sunk beneath an intolerable weight of aqueous salt. Ariel gasps, and retches; instantly his mouth takes in noxious water. This monstrous city, who placed it here? Who conceived this fetid place of human density, who cast it into the depths? Ariel, nominally the spirit of shipwreck, is sick with himself: this is my city, a city rank with sickness and salt, a city gone under: a thoroughly wretched place. What have I done? What have I made, and what is this man going to write? Ariel would weep for himself were he not floating already in a sea of stale tears. The word comes to him in a salty nauseous wave, the name of this city, which he knew from Sunday school and promptly forgot with the rest of history, the city sunk by wrath beneath the weight of the Dead Sea: Gomorrah.

Izzy pays for his coffee and departs. The waitresses say good-bye to every other customer, but not to him. "Bye, babe. Bye . . ." To Izzy, nothing. They whisper among one another.

He turns back onto Charlton; the crane is gone. Not knowing what he hopes to see, Izzy looks up six stories to his apartment window: there is no printing press. No hole. The wall is intact, the window closed. Inexplicably saddened, he unlocks the front door and enters the gray, prisonlike corridor. Behind him, from across the street, a young boy with a gashed forehead stares.

A tiny red diode on his answering machine is flashing insistently to indicate a message lying dormant. Nobody calls Izzy. Ever. The actors do not have his number. He does not have friends in this city. Nervous, Izzy Darlow presses the button to access his new message. The tape rewinds. It continues to rewind. This message is long. Izzy lifts the cover on the tape to watch it spin: the message takes up his entire tape. Somebody has been speaking into his machine for half an hour, while he was at the coffee shop. At last, the tape judders to a halt, spins slowly forward, and a voice emerges from the gray box:

"Izzy? Izzy Darlow? Is this Izzy Darlow, from Toronto? I've been told to call you . . ."

The voice is feminine, poised, oddly focused, as if the young woman were speaking while looking into a telescope. "My name is Arianna. I live in my father's house. You can help me, I think."

Izzy Darlow does not know any woman named Arianna.

"You can help me. And I can help you. I have pieces of the story that you need. I can help you put it all together, plan and build it, and then . . . I can help you find your way out. Maybe you don't believe me. Maybe you don't trust me. I can be trusted, Izzy Darlow. I have what you need."

And then, as if to offer proof, the voice begins to relate, in a voice even more abstract—as if telling a tale to a small child—the following story.

PART TWO: SECTION

I feel that biography as a form has become the revenge of little people on big people. Little people who have little lives are able to condescend to those who are superior to them by saying, "He was a cruel father," and so on.

—EDMUND WHITE, GENET'S BIOGRAPHER

TALLNESS

A study of Ariel Price is, of necessity, a study of gesture. Grand, sweeping gesture, in its own way as important in the history of twentieth-century art as the painterly urge that moves a drunken symbolist to abandon figurative concerns and dribble ordinary house paint across unstretched canvas.

The gesture toward height is perhaps the most famous and unambiguous of these: every first-year student of architecture learns, and receives with awe, that it is Ariel Price who made the city tall. Certainly, in the history of the skyscraper there are earlier bold innovations, later twists and refinements, but the theoretical thrust—the celebration of tallness itself as an instrument of urban density, and verticality as the primary orientation of urban flow—this can be ascribed only to the genius of the early Price.

A gesture perhaps less marked, because less immediately visible, is to my mind the more important, however, in the understanding not simply of the Price oeuvre, but the way in which that work grows inextricably from the life: the gesture toward depth.

It is Ariel Price who first banishes the urban mall to the dark places beneath the street.

This move, in itself, constitutes a fundamental change in attitude. Others have argued that the creation of the sub-city is simply a means of cleaning up the landscape, of clearing the ground plane for the placement of crystalline lobbies against the emptiness of plaza and street, but I shall argue, from the begin-

ning of this biography, that it is something more. It is a recognition of a new cosmological picture. It is, in built form, the celebration of Romantic Nature. It is precisely analogous to the boy poets' love for, and apotheosis of, the bold but tragic figure of Satan: the elevation of Hell over Heaven. It is, in other words, a revolution.

I shall demonstrate as well that, like both Prometheus and Satan, like all true revolutionaries, the great figure of Ariel Price emerges in history only through the perpetration of an arrogant, and unspeakable, crime.

It was a cold September day, otherwise undistinguished, in the early stages of Mr. Price's sojourn in the forsaken city of Toronto, that he first looked out into the gray plaza to see a young girl dancing in front of a paper cup filled with coins . . .

The distinguished Ariel Price had rented an office on the second floor of the Letztesmann Tower. He was not pleased with the level of his office. The second floor should not by rights exist in a Pricean tower, except as cathedral ceiling in the expanse of lobby. But this was an unambitious building, sketched by a famous Toronto modernist whose sole claim to prominence seemed to be the inclusion of bits of Canadian Shield in loose mosaic patterns on the walls.

Ariel Price had taken this office so that he could personally oversee the digging of the foundations across the way: he was designing the new Letztesmann Tower, after which the building in which he worked would be torn down. It was the tenth anniversary of the death of Herschel Letztesmann, a beloved mayor, and the new tower was to be raised in his honor.

The old Letztesmann Tower had a little plaza appended to the west wall, a designated public space, which for some reason the public avoided assiduously. In winter the winds would blow great drifts of snow up against one edge of the space and eddies of loose powder would skirl over the sludge in the middle, in the spring the plaza would be emptied in favor of the tiny urban parkettes, and in summer it would bake and crack beneath an intolerable sun. Now, at the onset of fall, the inadequate drainage had made most of the plaza into an inch-deep pool, stagnant and filthy with leaves. Why the young girl had chosen this, the Letztesmann Plaza, as a performance space, Ariel Price could not determine. It was simultaneously heartbreaking and enchanting, the guileless choice of this sad deserted theater. Ariel knew from watching that none of the coins in the soggy cup were thrown there by ardent admirers; he was as far as he could tell the only ardent admirer; he had seen the girl empty a cloth purse into the cup before beginning her desperately cheerful routine.

The act of watching, surreptitious watching, breeds an approximation of love. It is the process by which, for instance, the reader grows enamored of a vicious protagonist. (Beware.) Ariel Price watched the girl through the one-way mirror of his office window, himself unwatched, and something stirred in the grand reptilian heart: something reptilian.

And it was here, dancing in the cold perfect eye of a lizard, that young Bethany revealed to heightened advantage all of the subtle ordinary human traits that made her—that make all human beings, by virtue of their flaws—capable of being loved: these are the cracks that invite evil. Her face was pretty but irregular. Her complexion was still youthful, clear and almost unreal in coloration, but beginning to give way to the effects of a hard life: desperate lines around the mouth and eyes, an all-too-white substratum on which the colors of exertion read like fever. And her eyes pellucid and vulnerable to a fault. They took you in, those eyes, were an invitation to great and dangerous intimacy, let down all guard and illuminated, without softening, the terrible nakedness of the inner life. She danced poorly.

Ariel had the uncanny feeling that she could see him, that they had made contact and were communing silently with each other, but this could not be true. His window was a blue mirror to the outside world. He had stood in the Letztesmann Plaza and tried to look in. It was impossible. But every time she inclined her head upward and in his direction, the limpid openness of her expression left him with the distinct sensation that she was responding to his stare.

Her chestnut hair was parted without a fringe and would occlude her face as she danced. She would brush it back impatiently with a quick movement of her hand, but it would return to blind her and add to her parcel of small and beautiful deficiencies. Ariel Price, coldly professional in even the most creative act, was, for the first time in his life, utterly charmed.

He had come from Berlin at the invitation of the municipal government to design and build the tallest and most elegant tower in the country, in honor of their dead, beloved mayor. The foundations were to be completed before the ground froze. Already they were digging deeply in the earth west of the Letztesmann Plaza. Ariel Price knew what the tower would be like— all of his towers were stylistically indistinguishable—but he had not yet solved crucial problems at the street level: how would the building address the ground plane, the Letztesmann Plaza, the pedestrian alleys between the existing towers? Circulation was, in the last analysis, everything, and he wanted to get it right.

The office looked out over the proposed site, and Ariel would sit there for hours, staring at the fenced lot and wondering what he could do to enhance the placement of the lobby, in order to fix, permanently, his preeminent position in the pantheon of rigorous modernists.

Lately, the daily appearance of Bethany in the plaza had derailed his serious contemplation. It was difficult to concentrate upon matters of linear and material perfection, with this imperfect but charming gypsy performing her graceless dance in his line of vision. *Damn her to hell.*

Izzy Darlow is unsurprised at this turn of events. Surely the architect would have to meet the young girl. Always, the architect must meet the young girl. While listening to Arianna's voice on his machine, Izzy Darlow inches down the corridor toward his northern room. He is frightened of what he may find there. The wall is healed. No trace of the infernal machine. The floor, however, is knee-deep in wet paper, curling about his feet. For reasons that he does not understand Izzy is relieved to find it there; he picks up a strand, and examines it. Later, he will not be able to remember which parts of the story he reads from the print drying on the wet paper, and which parts are announced, in the voice of an unknown woman, from the tape in his front room.

Why did the dancing girl return, day after day? Ariel had never seen anyone give her a coin. He had never seen anyone stop for more than a moment before dismissing the amateur performance with a sad shake of the head. Was she practicing? Was she shy?

It was, in a sense, irresponsible to permit the foundations to be dug before he had resolved crucial details of the tower in his mind, but his reputation was such that he was not to be questioned, and it was something of a game with him to put himself in this kind of position: a theoretical labyrinth from which he could extricate himself only by way of a concentrated, virtuoso performance. It was a test of the nerves and a proof of the artist.

And this was getting in the way: it had been years since his work was last confused by strong emotion.

"Do not feel. Build." That pithy twin commandment had been widely anthologized. His American students always responded well to short phrases: it was not that they shared a modern disposition, an appreciation of the clean, the minimal, the perfect—on the contrary, the American aesthetic was baroque and tending toward the grotesque—no, it was a peculiar national attribute, an intellectual deficiency that seemed to go hand in hand with eagerness and industry: the attention span of a lesser mammal. And god knows there was enough feeling in the air. It could fuel a bulky romance, the cheap emotion that fluttered over the drafting tables in his American classes.

Of course, Ariel Price felt indebted to the American psyche. It threw up so few obstacles. Specifically, he rarely had to fight a nostalgic attachment to the old—there was no old—so he had little difficulty persuading civic elders to raze the city core in favor of the new. Canada was, if anything, even easier. There was a voracious emptiness here, a vacuumlike need for what was termed "culture." Ariel could not relate to this concept of culture: the word for him had centuries of layered associations; it was woven through the fact of life; it was like the word "thought" or "landscape."

This is perhaps one reason that it distresses him so greatly when Theseus Crouch designates him (with pages of supporting evidence): "the most complete barbarian of the age."

But now, staring out over the Letztesmann Plaza, Ariel Price was not yet sixty, and he had not yet encountered his biographer; he had not yet contemplated, seriously, the notion that he might die and become subject not simply to interpretation, but judgment. Such thoughts were decades distant, and for the moment he merely felt, like a painful debilitating sickness, the growing paralysis of lust.

Sometimes it is not enough to look at the surface of a thing. Sometimes it is painful. An architect, in particular: an architect wants to know more. A girl dancing, clothed, will never satisfy the eye; every dance is the Dance of the Seven Veils.

It is a little-known fact of the Price life—not even Theseus Crouch will unearth this delicate episode—that the young architect turned, for a time, to the study of dressmaking. Toward the end of his life Price would look at this foray as an act of adolescent madness: it grew out of an obsession with nakedness, and how best to clothe an object so that it remained essentially nude. A girl, Price determined, would be at her most pure—at her most exposed—in a white dress. And a building, too: the facade of a building would best reveal the structure beneath if clothed in white.

Signus Writhe, a theorist and prodigy, will publish his thesis months after Crouch's death, confirming Writhe as the foremost authority in Price studies (while Crouch himself gradually turns to anonymous dust). "Ariel Price, Cross-Dressing Patriarch," a slim but elegant paper, will dwell upon the Price obsession with clothing, and will argue persuasively that the most famous of the late Price drawings—the great section through the Letztesmann Tower—is in effect a sublimated effort to strip the clothing from the urban corpus, to render the city naked.

And, remarkably, Writhe will come to this conclusion without the benefit of Crouch's biographical discovery: Price's encounter with the dancing girl.

Ariel's young assistant, Cosimo, stood at his shoulder as he watched the girl dance. "She's not very good, is she. Pretty, in a way, but not very good . . ."

"Shut up." This hideous assistant, assigned to him without consultation, made him twitch. The boy could draw, certainly, and he had ideas, but he was physically deformed. First in his class at the University of Toronto School of Architecture—all very well—but one arm was longer than the other, and the boy limped, and his face was villainous. The teeth protruded from twisting lips, the hairline receded irregularly as a result of a massive birthmark over the scalp, and everything conspired to abort symmetry: one eye was lower than the other, one nostril larger, one gibbous shoulder pressed against the neck as if the boy were trying to hold a telephone while typing. Nauseating.

Who are you to cast judgment on the physique of this charming girl? He wanted to say this, but did not. The boy was useful.

Cosimo flinched, and was silent. He had known in advance—he had read it in textbooks—that Mr. Price would be a difficult and demanding master, less polite than his Canadian teachers. What he could not yet understand, however, was how the brusque manner of the great architect did not seem to conceal any real desire to teach. When his father had berated him for clumsiness, it had been understood that Cosimo was being prepared for the world, that the treatment, however painful, was motivated by affection. Cosimo had no doubt that Ariel Price, a legendary architect, would possess far greater depths of humanity than a rough construction worker one generation removed from a small Calabrian village, but he had yet to discover any sign of it.

Cosimo was born to learn, but it had always been difficult to play the student. A Canadian teacher would require, simultaneously, the rebellious attitude that gave rise to good work, and the subjection to authority that reinforced the teacher's sense of self. It was a balancing act, an effort to preserve authenticity between acts of hypocrisy. His physical complaints made it somewhat easier; there was pity. A truly repulsive face could never erode a teacher's confidence the way that youthful beauty inevitably did. Nevertheless, Cosimo's views were so strong that he found himself, no matter how hard he tried to mediate his delivery, always on the edge of outraging his mentors.

The weeks with Ariel Price were utterly different. The great architect seemed unmoved by pity. Certainly, he was aware of Cosimo's deformities, but they in themselves seemed to constitute for Ariel an outrage against order: an affront. As for Cosimo's ideas, Ariel Price had a certain amount of respect for attainment and ambition, but he was not in the least interested in what a young student of architecture might have to say.

Cosimo was expected to absorb the master's process. He was to remain silent and copy the famous details until he could produce, himself, effortless examples of Pricean work.

Cosimo never had to worry about the seduction of mediocrity; compromise was never an option. Whenever his work failed to please him he was overcome with revulsion, a sickness at becoming the conduit for something less than acceptable, and he would naturally right himself like a sailboat after a squall. This had nothing to do with moral concerns or any theory of correct artistic behavior. It was simply the way he was made.

The giving over of himself to Ariel Price was humiliating but did not revolt him. Though he was not producing his own work when he slavishly copied Price's techniques, he was producing acceptable work, and this kept revulsion at bay. Nevertheless, there was a psychological tide rising in Cosimo Neri; he was swelling toward something ineluctable, and the force of his ideas would soon carry him up and over even the tutelage of Ariel Price. For the truth was, at the core, Cosimo was an enemy of the modern age.

When Cosimo studied the course that his art had taken in this, his century, at every major juncture he found himself questioning, pursuing the branching path, forsaking the real. Dangerous questions, delirious paths, silent rebellion: what if some idiosyncratic genius, obsessed with human scale, ornament, and regional personality, had eclipsed the nascent International Style? In other words, what would cities look like if Ariel Price were irrelevant?

He carried these questions with him in silence, as he detailed matching marble slabs for the Price tower.

But he was cautious around the great man, and when Ariel told him to shut up—however inappropriately and without apparent motive—he shut up. The girl dancing in the square was a poor dancer; nothing Ariel Price could say would alter that fact; but similarly, nothing Cosimo could say would add anything to the truth of it. Beauty was beauty, and required neither justification nor championship: it just was.

Partially it was Cosimo's equanimity that infuriated Ariel. How could a creature so obviously inferior in every way be so sure of himself? As appalled with himself as he was to find the young dancer clouding his introspection with vaporous desires, so was he annoyed to find the atmosphere of his office tainted with uncontrollable loathing.

Something would have to give.

After a fortnight of watching, during which the tower progressed so slowly that the clients were beginning to have reservations about the great man, Ariel decided to take his lunch in the square. He purchased a turkey sandwich on white bread from the foreign lady who ran a shop off the lobby, had her wrap it in brown paper, and carried it out into the Letztesmann Plaza with a small bottle of grapefruit juice.

The girl was dancing, as always. Ariel sat rigidly on a slim concrete bench directly in front of the girl, who hopped nervously from one foot to the other and did her best not to meet his eyes. He smiled an agitated smile that tried to look satisfied and patronizing, but increasingly resembled a predatory leer. He tore at the sandwich with his teeth.

For a man almost sixty, Ariel had an uncommonly youthful face. His hair had been white from his mid-twenties, at which time he seemed strangely old for his years, but he had not visibly aged much since then, and could still pass for a man of perhaps thirty or forty. His features were cinematic, almost hyperbolic: the angles of his face cut angry shadows in a camera lens. And he had gravitas, a very European attribute, an ancient way of carrying himself that seemed faintly ludicrous in North America—he looked as if he ought to be wearing a toga. All of this combined to unnerve the poor dancing girl almost completely.

He smiled as he chewed his turkey.

You can help me, Izzy Darlow. I know that you have never helped anyone before, in your peculiar life, but I am alone here, in my father's house, and you can help me.

From no precise point does the public square form a perfect rectangle. There is distortion. Even from the perfect vantage point, equidistant from the sides and suspended high in the air, the edges curve to fit the lens. They do, though you cannot see them; the mind always compensates. Even when you force yourself to be aware of perspective (and how often do you do this?) you cannot see the way the straight lines curve. Some things you do not want to see. They put fear into the everyday.

Cosimo, who was surprised to find Ariel Price absent from the office—the great man would insist upon the entire staff taking lunch at their desks—glanced out the window and discovered, with a shock of mixed emotions, Herr Price on his bench and the young girl, dancing in his vision, impaled there like a fish squirming on a spear.

From the ideal vantage point, suspended above the square, the lines of sight come together like vectors, lines of desire with force and direction: Ariel, Bethany, Cosimo.

When the architect stood to place a penny in the cup, the girl stopped dancing, grabbed the cup and prepared to dart from the plaza. Ariel held out his penny and smiled. Bethany cringed and froze, a deer in a headlight, her face twisted with revulsion. Ariel ceased to smile, and Cosimo went pale.

The pattern of forces shines with a new and mysterious tendency. It burns like the light through a crystal, focused and geometrically profound; the simple pattern coheres hard and bright and eternal and becomes the inevitable seed, the acorn at the core, the beginning of the ineluctable course of events: the dread narrative.

This is the genesis of plot. The story will grow outward in rings.

Without waiting for her penny—the architect approaches— the girl Bethany ran. Ariel stood. Cosimo saw the expression on the architect's face, and shivered: slowly, and with great malice, the great man smiled.

Ariel Price had resolved in his mind the problem of the mall.

There comes a point in any monumental task, where the once easy path drops away like a cliff. For me, in the reconstruction of this biography, the point was reached at the beginning of my attempt to research the most austere and famous of Price's late projects: the tombstone-like Letztesmann Tower, which for many years dominated the funereal skyline of Toronto.

Nobody knew anything about this tower. The documents, where they existed, were occult. The witnesses were strangely absent. I spent some time trying to hunt down Price's crippled assistant on the project—a young man named Cosimo Neri, who by all accounts showed the promise of a shining career—but he seemed to have disappeared. Certainly he had never made the impact upon the profession that early indications of talent would have suggested.

The path, up until then a bewildering wealth of information, simply vanished. There was nothing. It was as if a whole segment of the great life had not been lived. And yet, in mute refutation of this, was the great tower itself. It stood. And beneath it, now widening to encompass the entire downtown core, was the notorious underground mall . . .

My father built this house. My father is an architect. He built this house especially for me. It is horrible. All I ask is your hospitality, Izzy, that you treat me with the kindness appropriate to a guest. I can tell you many things. Please be kind to me.

Cosimo pulled the crippled shell of his body into the public space. For most people, he knew, carriage was not an issue: some were concerned, perhaps, about posture, what kind of figure was cut by their presence, but few worried literally about how their body was carried on its frame. It took a particular division from the self—a looking back at oneself from ahead, a looking down from above, the distance of contemplation when the object is viewed with purest horror—to carry the body, consciously, the way that Cosimo carried his: as if it were a carcass, stolen, slung over his shoulder.

The distance of contemplation. When the phobic views a

spider, there is a moment, always, when the soft down of the abdomen is felt against the cornea, and then a moment, in this dialectic of vision, when the actual distance between the phobic and his object of lust is magnified almost to the point of vertigo and the spider becomes a distant image as if viewed through the wrong end of the telescope, jiggling at the end of the optical path, and then—for every two moments of horror begets a necessary third—there is the moment when the distance between the phobic and his darling is precisely the distance between Narcissus and his virtual image, and in the self-loathing that frightens the eyes from focus, two human eyes spread darkly across the field of vision, flowering into eight.

Cosimo saw himself from precisely this distance, across the Letztesmann Plaza his body hauled as if it were the bloated abdomen of a spider.

It always fascinated him, this division from self. He had read with a quickening heart that Shelley, the vicious poet, when a boy would stare down at himself as if from a great height in the text of his letters: Shelley, the scheming spider of adolescence, caught in a web of sticky symbols, drowned much later in a boat whose very name called up the spirit of going under. Izzy Darlow, in a story as yet untold, would walk across this same square and see himself reflected in his own eyes, too wrapped up in self-love and self-loathing to see the shining head tilted forward across the sky, gazing down at him with the blue eyes of the puppeteer. But Cosimo looked up. Our eyes met. You are my cripple and I am your imperfect creator. From the ideal vantage point, suspended above the square, Cosimo seems to have but two human eyes, and yet he saw himself reflected in the mild blue eyes above him as the slow and hungry creature of eight. The strings that bound him to the puppeteer seemed, from this perspective, the web of another spider: the web that had caught even him.

Shivering slightly, Cosimo looked down again and made his way. The walls about him fused with strong amber light, light become stone, the color of dying sun so much stronger, strangely, than the sun at the top of its arc—all things writhe in dying with the strength of the drowning man—he cast a sharp and long shadow, an incision in the surface of the pavement. A child somewhere unseen repeated a phrase of nonsense, over and over again, like steps toward madness, and Cosimo carried himself through the light and mantra of this, the closing day.

A green vehicle hummed across the periphery of his vision, sucking garbage from the floodlit pavement. He remembered with satisfaction his first architectural project, in which he had designed the vehicle of revelation: a simple passenger bus, descending toward a city condemned. It satisfied him, because it seemed to him the beginning of a story, one that would carry him through a life of creation. Despite the horror that waited at the end of the journey. It had been a long time since he had had the luxury to concentrate upon his own work—Ariel Price ran him like a slave—but he would think back upon his own projects at the end of the day with a smile: there was much to go back to. It would be a terrible thing indeed if his own life of making were pulled entirely into the vortex of Ariel Price and his voracious career, if Cosimo's own story were to become a mere episode, or worse, a skeletal image of the full and vile body of Price and his solid buildings. He shuddered. Surely something else can matter, despite existing in the path of great men?

Cosimo carried his weary frame across the Letztesmann Plaza, feeling in his skin the unliving concrete around him, florid with dying light, and then he sensed—as one does—another creature, close by, sentient and perceptive: a mind with a world of its own, sharing the dead space with his shameful body.

Lying beneath the stone bench, and shivering from hunger, was the frail form of a young dancing girl.

Ariel Price, staring out the window, took note of all that occurred, drew a small line on a torn piece of vellum, and filed the business away under the words: crippled assistant encounters girl in plaza—generative concept for the plan of an underground mall. It amused him the way that even the smallest life could be made a piece of the work.

The author, pondering the digital files that constitute his unfinished book, wonders: what is he trying to make?

It seemed, just pages ago, something striving to be tall, a towering structure, a book that incorporates many lives into its fabric the way that a tower cradles lives on every floor, but this seems hardly possible, now. And surely there is something to be said for the opposite urge: the wish to make something small, and authentic, and human. A girl beneath a concrete bench, thinking small but human thoughts, the world of her mind. There is nothing unambitious about this urge, nor politically suspect; there is a kind of greatness in the concerted effacement of glory; it need not lead us to the failed experiments of this century, the will to mediocrity, no. For there is tyranny in that direction, too, and this small project seems to be, if nothing, else, a thing made in the face of tyranny. And if I can do this, thinks the author, keep the small but essential human soul, the single soul, the soul of the individual, somehow flickering and alive in the wind of architectonic arrogance and the tide of collective nihilism, I will have made something of worth.

And do not underestimate the terrible effort that such making requires. The small self is always in danger of being lost; it is a subtle thing; its life flickers just this side of violence; it is so easily extinguished. And never again to be revived. It is a small thing.

Cosimo Neri, talented cripple, extended a soft hand to the young girl shivering beneath the concrete bench.

The girl felt Cosimo's touch, and opened her eyes, then closed them with revulsion. Is my weakness merely this: an invitation to monsters? But there was something in the texture of his skin that was different: it seemed tremulous, careful and alive, as if it were capable of judging the difference between fine and less fine paper—and of course it could—and Bethany opened her eyes again to meet the eyes of the bent student who had touched her.

"Are you cold?"

The girl nodded, closing her eyes again.

"Hungry?"

She continued to nod.

"Come with me. We'll get something to eat."

The eyes opened, a little bit wet now, like sexual organs. "I just want something small. Something small. Not expensive. Okay?"

"Sure. We'll get soup and bread and pasta, it's cheap. Come with me."

The girl stood, swaying slightly, and Cosimo made to catch her should she sicken and fall, but she did not. She clung to his arm with one strong hand, and he felt new strength radiating from the bruise that she made: she will hurt me with need, this girl. They walked together, Cosimo with great care, and Bethany with deliberate but faltering steps, and for the first time in his life Cosimo was not the cripple.

He took her onto the streetcar, and as it lurched into motion she fell against him, and stayed there, her head against his shoulder almost as if she were in love with him, except that a thin trickle of spit descended from her mouth and wet his shirt in a spreading stain: it was nothing but weakness.

He took her up the stairs to his second-floor apartment; they stopped on the landing to gather strength; he left her sprawled on his mattress as he shopped for food. Cosimo returned quickly, almost running, because it seemed impossible to him that she would not disappear in his absence. Some things were not meant to be, and a woman laid out upon his mattress in an attitude of sex, or perhaps death or prayer, was not part of what was meant to be, and the painful and touching impossibility of it all might suddenly occur to the world and the world might be forced to take the moment back, to correct this moment with a sudden heaving and erasure: No, I'm sorry, but you were meant to be alone. And so he ran back with hard bread, and fresh pasta and artichokes and sun-dried tomatoes, and a plastic container heavy with clear soup.

She was still there when he returned. She had barely moved. They said nothing as he held a match over the gas and it sprung into blue hissing flame. He boiled water. He put the soup on the flame in a blackened pot. All in silence. At last she spoke, in a quiet and sickly voice: "I thought you weren't going to come back."

Cosimo laughed, unhappily. "And I thought you'd be gone."

When the soup was moving in its pot and giving off a cloud

of fragrant steam, he lifted it from the stove and poured some into a large coffee mug, which he carried to the bed. "Careful. It's very hot. I think you'll like it . . . I hope so . . . it's pretty good, I think . . . here."

She sat up against the wall, and went pale with the effort, then took the cup from his hands.

"Thank you . . ."

"Don't burn yourself . . ."

"Thank you."

And with the first sip she retched and let the soup fall and splash against the mattress, burning Cosimo's leg, and she curled into a ball, away from him, ashamed, and began to cry. "I'm sorry, I'm so sorry . . . Oh god . . . I'll never be able to live . . ."

Cosimo said nothing, but picked up the cup, wiping it carefully. He filled it again at the stove, and carried it back to Bethany on the bed. She held on to it, staring at him as if he were a miracle—nobody had given her this much care and patience in some years—and as she put the cup to her lips, he ran a finger through her hair, then pulled it back, going red. She swallowed a small amount of soup this time, with difficulty, then put the cup aside. She took Cosimo's hand and put it to the side of her head, which was wet with sickness. Cosimo leaned forward to kiss her on the forehead, and he could smell the fever in her hair.

"You're sick . . ."

"You're kind."

"No I'm not. I'm not. I'm . . . hideous, really. Hideous, and a bit lonely, and I'm taking advantage of your weakness to touch you. It's not kindness. And it wouldn't be kindness if I drugged some little girl and raped her . . ."

"Stop it."

He backed away from her, but she caught him in her strong hand.

"No, I mean stop talking. You're saying foolish, stupid things." Bethany pulled him forward again. She closed her eyes, to prevent revulsion, and kissed the gnarled lip. "Just stop talking." She kissed him again; her mouth tasted sour; and then began to cry into his neck. "You're good . . . you're good . . . don't tell me anything else . . . I don't want to know . . ."

"Okay . . ."

"Just stop talking . . ." She kissed him again and again with the will to drive the loathing out of him, and Cosimo, despite himself, began to cry as well.

They sat for a long time on that mattress, confining themselves to the soft rectangular space and filling it with their conversation, haunting it, making it different with knowledge. And as the space changed around them, the sun charted its way through the last angles of falling toward the geometrical expression of disappearance. Darkness.

Their skin took on the faint, almost subliminal glow that white limbs evince as the eyes begin to find them in gloom; Cosimo and Bethany, developing like photographs, emerged slowly into each other's eyes.

Cosimo spoke abstractly, in measured and sophisticated phrases, as if telling a complex fairy tale to an adult child. He told Bethany many things, about shelter and the human need to build it, about the hierarchy of spaces that makes for ritual and depth, about the beginnings of architecture, barely perceptible beneath the ink of legend: Daedalus and the labyrinth at Knossos, marvelous devices, the deception of kings. He spoke of all these things with reverence and care, because these were the topics that informed his life. Without them he was merely a cripple.

Bethany understood very little, but she knew that this story made sense of him, told Cosimo as if he were an anecdote; she too had encountered a tale, once, that had woven her into the greater narrative, given her purpose, marked her trajectory from despair to meaning.

Cosimo spoke for many hours. It was a way of denying the body.

Izzy Darlow, seated in the midst of the tortuous scroll in his northern room, becomes suddenly aware—with a deep feeling of loss—that the answering machine has come to the end of its tape. The message is finished. The voice is gone.

Can you fall in love with a voice? How much of the soul is body? Izzy Darlow knows, as well as anyone, the complications arising from corporeal passion, how the blood in the body as it takes in oxygen and goes from milky blue to that other color, called "blood," breathes into it the dangerous substance of life: air that includes the breath of other human beings and the possibility of eros. Izzy does not know how powerful, yet, a voice alone may be, but he knows well that the flesh can incite madness, can turn a linear life away from its reasoned path and send it cycling into misery, the distortion of memory, paramnesia. This woman, however, Arianna, is only a voice. Magnetic. Mere voice without presence, the shape of breathing without the scent and feel of breath. And yet Izzy Darlow misses her already.

For a long moment he sits, the waves of paper breaking against his body, and wonders what he will do with the long message on his answering machine, the text even longer winding about his legs and arms. Can he make something of this? He wishes with surprising intensity that the voice on his machine would return, and contemplates rewinding the tape and listening to the message from the beginning, in its entirety.

But he knows that this is futile. A voice changes when it is heard a second time. It ceases to announce itself, and becomes mere recording. Once he took a naked picture of a woman that he loved, but the picture offered him nothing when she was gone: it haunted him, cried with absence, became no longer a picture of her but a photograph of loss. He put it away in a deep drawer, and even there it made him unhappy, until he had to burn it.

This tape may well do the same.

Izzy sits, wondering how he can make his way through the silence, now that the voice is gone: he picks up a strand of paper, a different strand, and begins to read:

Tom Sorrow passed through the curtain wall and approached the white shaft that housed the elevators. Here in the Letztesmann Tower he was prepared to change the course of his life, to fight those demons that so often prevented worthy men from attaining their true wealth.

The white core of the tower beckoned, gleaming, a pillar of salt. Through this stone spine ran the mighty elevator that would take the aspiring wealth-seeker to the floor of his assignment, to meet with men who had taken the great wealth-seeking path before him and had succeeded in that heroic voyage.

The hush of the lobby was immense. Tom stopped for a moment, and took in the sound of it: the sound of a marble floor as it met a flawless wall of marble, the sound of perfection. He made a fist, stared at it and smiled, shaking his head proudly. It was a good fist. The elevators—whole glorious banks of them—winked open and shut like the eyes of angels, like the parting of the clouds that permits, for a moment, access to the glorious sun-drenched firmament, that permits a sole ray of straight and perfect hope to pierce the wealth-denying gloom and illuminate the forgotten crust of the earth. The silence of these winking eyes, almost lewd in their promise.

One bank of elevators promised to take him all the way to the Penthouse. He liked that. Here was a mechanical construct that echoed, in its ambition, his own irrepressible sense of the great pattern: that proud things rose very high indeed.

Tom pressed a button. Although it was by no means time for him to make his debut in the Penthouse, Tom pressed the top button, simply for the pleasure that the pressing of such a button might afford. He saw, down the road, whole years during which he would press that button lawfully: during which that button would mark his place in the world, would be his address.

The button lit up, with a soft, ethereal glow. And then— Tom had almost allowed himself to forget, in the passion of his act, that the pressing of buttons has consequences—the great hanging vehicle began to ascend.

He was on his way to the top floor. Nothing to be done. Yes, he might have pressed some intermediate button, some minor floor number interposed between him and that lofty destination, but he rejected this alternative as symbolic of cowardice: if one aspires to the Penthouse, one aspires to the Penthouse.

The elevator climbed with silent but perceptible speed, the very quality of the air against his ears changing with the altitude.

His stomach fluttered in its cage of muscle like a quivering bird. A tiny, eloquent device above the door listed the floors as he flew by: 1, 2, 3, 4 . . .

He was soon high above the city, and still rising: god the achieve of, the mastery of the thing!

And then, for all such flights must come to an earthly conclusion, lest the traveler find himself propelled upward without limit to the very throne of god, Tom's elevator came to a quiet but wrenching stop.

The letter P shone in the window of that eloquent device, and it was clear to Tom that this letter was an abbreviation for the place at the threshold of which he now stood: the Penthouse. The door, dual in its aspect, opened.

Even Tom, primed and proud and irrepressible in his heroic trajectory, felt a brief panic as the Penthouse widened into view. What was he doing here? What would he say? This was no ordinary floor, but the Penthouse of the Letztesmann Tower: once the very highest floor in the city of Toronto.

What first occurred to the awed young man, as the Penthouse became apparent in the proscenium arch of his opened vehicle, was that day had given way, in his rising, to something else. There was no light on this floor. The Penthouse hovered, at the top of the building, in a kind of infernal gloom. For a moment, so dim was the vast room relative to the light in his elevator, Tom could see nothing. The elevator itself did not illuminate much: a faint trapezoid of light fell widening against the floor in front of him, but quickly bled into shadow.

Tom squinted. Vague shapes floated in front of his eyes. At last, when the eyes found their place in that spectrum, one shape among them became clearest, standing out against the darkness, dominating. A tall man, impossibly tall, with a shock of silvery white hair, leaned over a vast drafting table, his shoulders hunched and taut. The man faced away from the elevator, and Tom hoped his doors would close before this frightening apparition became aware of his intrusion. He jabbed at the "close doors" button with a nervous finger, but the doors remained frozen, and he in their frame, naked and exposed.

The man at the table slowly turned. His face was grave and long, sharpened with concentration and age, a grim, beautiful face. "Ja?" said the man, in a threatening voice.

"Um, hello," said Tom.

It was not so much that he finally ran out of things to say; Cosimo could have spoken for as long as Scheherazade, and for much the same reason; it was the need that arose through his speaking and the fear that abated. His hideous form diminished through the working of higher things. The space between them itself began to speak. Bethany touched the back of his hand.

Cosimo fell into silence, and for the first time in hours, looked at her. She touched his face, closing her eyes to his openness, reading his face like a blind woman. She shivered, with love and revulsion, and recognized in that moment that the two were, for her at this piece of her life, one and the same. Can I truly look at anyone without feeling this: appalled? And through the pall is love.

She moved her hands over his face, pressing with her fingertips, releasing; she found the scar of his lip, moved her fingers across it, found the distorted ridge of his eyebrow, traced it, moved into the horrible tangle of hair. Hanging about his neck with her full weight, which was small, Bethany let her head fall against the sharp bone of his chest. She found a place there, and breathed.

Cosimo reached his hands up tentatively and held them inches from her fevered hair, cradling the air about her for a terrible moment, then plunging: he touched her small and perfect ear, traced the seashell edge of it, listened to her breathing alter and wondered about the precise import of this change. What are we doing to each other?

And as the sun examined the impossible myriad of lives, teeming in dwellings and fields and roads on the other side of the blue planet, two quivering souls pulled the gloom around each other to hide the revulsion that stands in the way of love, and they stripped the clothing from each other as if it were bandages, carefully and with great concern, and soon their bodies were wet with the tears that the skin will shed when the eyes are closed and the anguish is indistinguishable from ecstasy.

From the vantage point of the reader, who has the luxury of muting the visual imagination, the vileness of Cosimo's physical self fades to insignificance and the soul itself fills the screen of the mind, transcendent and purged of death. And the reader imagines that Bethany herself has accomplished this, an act of sacred denial, and that her urgent and now urgently breathing nakedness is, for her, at the level of something other than body, though her breathing is hard and has a cry in it: no, which means no to everything in the world but him.

For a small eternity the two combine in the skylike darkness, obscured from and separated from and no longer tied to the bodies that pursue their slow progress of decay on the mattress below.

The body examines in love every age of man: the wondering

helplessness of the child, the violent urgency of adolescence, slowing to the sadness of routine, and then the crisis as death nears, the slackening of all function, and sleep.

And should the reader choose to look hard on the lovers, he would see, briefly, the entire cycle of transformation in the bodies themselves: the movement from the womb into the sun and strength and the terrible decay that brings flies from the air and curls flesh blackly from the bones and leaves everything glittering white in the road. And then it is over.

Cosimo and Bethany stared at each other, breathing lightly. She took a wet arm and tried vainly to wipe the wet salt from his forehead, and laughed.

The plot has survived its first great catastrophe.

Izzy Darlow looks up from his page, but before he can properly digest this turn in the path of the narrative, an angry noise, like a machine dying, erupts at the end of his corridor. Always this noise comes to him first as a terrifying surprise, and his mind scurries about its reptilian regions to identify the source— breaking mechanism, factories collapsing, looms sabotaged— but it is only the buzzer, too loud and almost broken, indicating a visitor at his front door.

This too is strange, however. Nobody visits Izzy Darlow. He walks huddled into the front room and presses the button— the one that ostensibly permits him to listen—and a voice erupts, mediated and mangled, from the tiny box. He cannot tell whether the voice is male or female, human or something else. The only words he can make out are: "cold . . . please . . . here . . ."

And then: "Arianna."

He presses the button marked "enter."

The story continues, silently, in the other room.

The young woman—for she was young, despite the deathly pale makeup that obscured the pink of her skin, like a mask—stared into her small pocket mirror and concentrated, drawing with immense care a perfect new mouth, black lipstick. She licked the upper lip, and the soft and human pink of her tongue made a nice little grotesque against the severe mask. She pursed her lips, kissing the air, then smiled. For years she had concentrated on purging warmth from that smile, and now it radiated precisely the degree of friendly malice that she imagined was in her heart: pure mischief. Scilla was not cold, precisely, but she was not warm.

"Spare change?" Although she was standing in line at the bank—an indication that she had an account, and therefore, money—Scilla was not above panhandling: it had nothing to do with need; it was a game. The tiny man whom she had hit upon regarded her with barely veiled disgust.

"Why don't you get a job."

"I have one." Scilla smiled. "I'm a babysitter. Do you have any children?" She licked her lips, and let her eyes widen.

The little man shuddered visibly as he turned away. Scilla leaned over, carefully, and planted a black kiss on the man's neck. He spun around, outraged, and raised a hand to strike her.

"*S'il vous plaît*," said Scilla, who had studied French in high school. "I like pain."

After a period so long and anxious that Izzy wonders whether he has imagined the voice from his intercom, he hears a light knock against his door. He lives on the sixth floor, with no elevator; some take longer to climb than others. Izzy Darlow stares through the peephole, and the face that comes to him, bent by the lens, is the face of a young woman. He opens the door.

Her hair is long, an unnatural red that nevertheless occurs in nature, and seems all the more unreal against the milk of her face. She does not seem to comb the mass to the left, ever; it billows and snarls, tangled against her head like a storm. On the right she is sane. And her eyes a numinous blue, sad and intelligent; Izzy Darlow would give much to know what those eyes mean.

When she speaks, Arianna speaks with the same voice that he has heard on his machine.

"I'm sorry to intrude like this. I can leave if you like."

"No. No, don't."

The woman smiles, eyes widening with pleasure. She extends a white hand. "Arianna."

"I'm Izzy. But you know that."

"Hi, Izzy."

"How did you get my number?"

"We know someone in common. Let's not talk about that now."

"Okay . . . So, what do we talk about?"

Arianna shrugs. "I don't know. What do people talk about?"

"I barely remember."

"Me neither."

They stare at each other, sharing this: a moment of alignment. It is always unexpected.

"I live alone, and I'm not . . . social. Really." Izzy laughs bitterly at the understatement.

"I don't. Live alone. I live with my father, in the house that he built for us. But he has no time for me. I might as well live in solitary."

"Your father builds houses?"

"He designs them. He's an architect."

Izzy nods slowly.

Arianna frowns, perturbed. "It's not his story. I don't want you to think that. I'm not telling my father's story. Not really . . ."

She touches the edge of her perfect teeth with her thumb, testing the sharpness. "I could write about him if I wanted. I could say things. He's very famous. But I don't happen to have a high opinion of . . . memoirs."

"No?"

"My pain happens to be personal. Private. My father is not the best person, but that doesn't mean he deserves a biography. Not everyone deserves vivisection."

Tom Sorrow sat at his desk on the second floor. He stared through the wall of glass at the mirrored wall that confronted him, echoing not his own image, but the image of the glass interceding, and frowned. What had that encounter meant? The elevator doors had shut before the man with the silver hair had had a chance to say anything more: simply *Ja*, which Tom gathered, from his little knowledge of things European, meant "yes." And yet there was no doubt: Tom was disturbed.

Perhaps it was simply the quality of light in the Penthouse, which was not what he had expected. No, the books that Tom had read, about the heroic path toward self-realization and wholeness and truth, had never indicated this: that one ascended into shadow.

He bounced a pencil lightly against his green glass desk, rhythmically, until the small graphite tip broke and flew. And then he shook his head, violently, as if trying to dislodge a stubborn thought, and smiled. Enough of this—he was not by nature a brooding character—time to get on with it.

Corporate leasing. That was the glorious path. Tom saw himself as a facilitator, someone whose own overflowing spirit might prove a beacon to others, or at least a friendly atmosphere within which others might achieve, and what better way to express this cheerful talent than corporate leasing? Tom would find places for others to occupy. He would fill the empty spaces in the tall city, and in doing so, would improve lives, and garner wealth. It all seemed so simple.

And the simple equation that he would employ to great effect in his sales meetings was this (despite the recent disquieting encounter at the very top of the tower): the height of an address was the measurement of a man's worth. If you leased an elevated space, it was a sign of an elevated mind, an elevated ambition, and ultimately, an elevated salary. Everyone should want to rise—wasn't that the point?—and in rising, should want, quite literally, to occupy the higher ground. And that was where he, Tom, came in: he was a merchant of altitude.

It was an arduous task, the wooing of a new tenant. A kind of dance, like the circling of boxers, like the wary mutual regard of an architect and his stalking biographer . . . Tom shook his head again. What an absurd thought. This was indeed a strange day.

But it was arduous. A client could leave you hanging for months before making a decision, and even then the decision was not necessarily in your favor. Not necessarily. Tom knew this, though it was his first day on the job: they had told him this in training. It was his job, his subtle and profound task, to ensure that the lengthy process of thought that led to a decision was always imperceptibly weighted in his favor. Over the course of many meetings, Tom had to move the heavy mind of the client in such a way that the momentum carried it with an inevitable force into his, Tom's, domain. It was like chess; it was like poker; it was like researching the sexual crimes of a famous man. Jesus. Where did that come from? It must be the air in this office.

Tom was pleased to have been offered, right from the start, an office in the Letztesmann Tower itself—where the bulk of his clients would seek space—even though he knew the rumors: that the Tower was a sick building, that it took a toll upon the lives that were lived on its floors, that something in the building invaded the mind and the body and crushed, slowly, the vital force from the unwary occupant, squeezing him dry like an orange. Hell, it was only a rumor.

Tom tapped the pencil against the glass desk, the hollow wood tip, emptied like Gloucester's eye socket, making a dull noise.

He did not yet have a secretary. And so, before he got down to the day's calls, Tom decided that he would descend himself into the subterranean mall, in pursuit of coffee.

Occupying spaces. That was what the city made necessary; it was the whole of what Scilla concentrated upon. For a long time she had maintained an alliance with a fearsome young man— a brilliant young man, unreliable—and together they had filled the empty spaces in the city with theater. One piece in particular had established a mysterious reputation for the pair. Nobody was precisely sure that the piece had ever been performed—supposedly at midnight, in an abandoned subway station beneath Shuter Street—but the critics were unanimous: it should have been. Every now and then you would meet a citizen, often someone himself unreliable, muttering on a street corner, who would tell you that he had seen it, and that yes, it had changed his life forever. Most of these people had clearly been changed, but it was hard to imagine that the alteration had been for anything but the worse.

Always at the edges of gossip among the makers of theater, especially on Queen Street, was the rumor that Scilla and Campbell were going to do it again: occupy some unimaginable space, bring it alive.

Campbell had disappeared after that famous performance, and Scilla had not seen him for some years, but she felt that they were still partners. It was a metaphysical bond, much stronger than earthly presence, much stronger than love.

Of love, Scilla knew a great deal. She had specialized in her knowledge, and could not be said to know much about the kinder aspects of love, but she knew a great deal. She had seen the heart twist, like a body on a rope. She knew that the path of love was helical, and deep: the path of the sharp object that enters and turns in the shape of a gyre.

The exigencies of a life in dance and theater had made her cold to sentiment: she had seen, too often, the most powerful bonds between lovers evaporate mysteriously on closing night, the charged atmosphere gone. Words were to be memorized and spoken with feeling, but they in themselves indicated nothing more than the quality of the performance. Words did not run deep. Pain, now: pain ran deep. There was a place for authenticity in love, but it was a place whose entrance had a terrible price: the place of submission, of devotion, of slavery. And it was inextricable from the concept of theater. What was real on stage was real in love. Scilla truly believed this. She had seen it.

Certain women had always been drawn to pain, but now men, increasingly, heard the call. She noted this, in the course of her varied romantic career. Once she had sought out small women, the ones who made themselves open, immediately, their whole need shining clearly in the upward tilt of the head, the thrusting forward of the small body, the lack of defenses; but now, she found that men were equally prepared to lose themselves to this kind of love. She no longer made love to women; it was too easy; and the men were very much available.

Scilla parceled her life out between these two activities, theater and love, and found that there was barely the need for anything else. Her life was whole.

Occupying spaces. She thought on this as she walked down the row of vendors who lined the street, displaying silver to be put through the body. Leather. On a whim, she took the stairs down to the underground mall.

Arianna's entrance into Izzy Darlow's house rhymes, the way that words rhyme, with Tom and Scilla's simultaneous descent into the architect's mall, with Cosimo and Bethany's encounter.

Arianna does not appear ready to explain her presence, and Izzy does not force the issue. He is happy that she is there. He trusts her, and would trust her even if she had not invoked their shared acquaintance, still unnamed. She seems to want to talk about her father.

"Could you look at me?"

Cosimo frowned. "I'm not sure I know what you mean."

"Just look at me. Look at me and try to see something."

Cosimo looked. Bethany was shivering, and so small, with a sheet wrapped about her. The sheet was wet with perspiration and clung to her skin so that the sharp pieces of her body stood out, the fragile points birdlike and crying for flesh. Cover me, her body said: cover me, I am so close to the bones and dust that I will become; cover me so that I can live. That was what he saw first.

"Are you looking at me?"

"Shh."

And then, Cosimo with his understanding of form and meaning looked at the structure of things that lies beneath and between the body, the truth of this shivering girl, which is there in the points beneath the sheet but is deeper, somehow, of another kind and color than skin, or flesh, or bone, or marrow, or blood, even though it is in all of these. He saw the part of her that would remain with him long after the part of her that would die, would die. And he saw that the rest of her would die, perhaps soon.

"What do you see?"

"Shh."

And then, Cosimo with his eye for the line and number that makes an equation of matter, saw in Bethany the eternal shape of the human story. The story that makes its way from cunt to grave, crawling and walking and striving, two-armed and two-legged, and (until they are put out) two-eyed and seeing, the stumbling human creature, pathetic in its flesh but somehow perfect in its story: Cosimo saw this and knew that Bethany, however lost to him she would be in her birdlike flesh, would be with him until the end.

"Do you see something?"

Cosimo closed his eyes. "Yes, I do."

What Cosimo saw was the work of a future biographer. An evangelist. He saw the way in which the present would be refracted through the lens of retrospection. The way that pieces of the moment he was living would become fragments of a mystery to be interpreted later. Much later. From the vantage point of a man looking back, a man trying to capture the heat of this moment's breath, long after it had cooled and dispersed in the wide and expanding universe. Cosimo felt Bethany's breath hot against the back of his hand.

"What do you see?"

Cosimo saw the resentful scholar, vain Theseus Crouch, looking back on this warm breath and trying, from a vantage point removed by violence and death and indifference, to reconstruct that breath in words of special damnation.

PARALLEL LIVES

Theseus Crouch sat, terrified, in the library. It was not coming together. The books were multiplying about him, professors conspiring in their offices, and he was making no progress toward knowledge. Even here, at this inferior university—the only one that would accept him—Theseus had been marked as an ordinary student, bright but strangely unexceptional. One of his professors had gone so far as to explain to him, gently, that not everyone was cut out to be a scholar: it was a matter of disposition; some were naturally bookish and inquisitive. Theseus was perhaps the most intelligent student in his class, but the professors found him coarse, vicious, motivated in a manner too base for the delicate task at hand.

But Theseus Crouch was not one to be cowed. He knew the measure of his talent: he was eloquent, quick, and capable of great cruelty. Scholarship was a bloodless pursuit. Theseus would devote himself to a more dangerous game. Increasingly, there was a market for probing biography: not scholarship, but elevated gossip, the careful dissection and ruin of lives. And Theseus knew, better than most, the tender nature of the past. How easily certain revelations might drive a man to despair. He would be a biographer.

Ariel Price was unhappy. His first commission, and it was this: a vertical structure. Price had spent the summer working on a grand manifesto, a defense of the horizontal, but the client wanted a building that would make its presence felt on the skyline, a tall building. And the money was very good. Were he to publish his manifesto, his very first structure would prove a mockery of his principles.

The decision was not difficult. A man must eat. Ariel burned the manifesto—how easily words burned—and began work on a more worldly essay, on the nature of the relationship between architect and client. This piece would prove almost as much of a sensation as that first building. First, he took personal credit for the urge toward the tall: Ariel detailed in elaborate poetic terms a dream he had once had as an adolescent—a dream about tallness and a high window—and the words proved so forceful that later the architect would come to believe that he had actually had this dream, that it was part of his formation as an artist. But then, to cover the fact of compromise, Ariel investigated the degree to which the great architect should be influenced by the whims of his client, and decided that this influence was not itself a negative thing, given the moral complexities of the world. Ariel Price would become, in two quick strokes, the man who made the city tall, and the theorist who slyly identified the true nature of the professional designer: the architect, said Ariel Price, with urbane, self-deprecating wit, is a whore.

Let us, for a moment, cut to the center of this story. If you take a knife to this long tale, you will find at the marrow something rather simple: punishment. If you score the rind of this complex tale, and peel apart the two halves to reveal the bleeding core, you will find Ariel Price, at the end of his long life, forced to think back on the events that have led him to this prison.

When Cosimo returned to the Price office the day after his evening spent with Bethany, the atmosphere was changed.

Ariel, once dismissive, was now attentive. The cruelty of omission was changed now, into a cruelty of focus. Cosimo was under the eye of the architect, his every move triangulated and rendered in perspective, drawn and quartered in that expansive mind.

Ariel Price had witnessed the encounter. He had seen his assistant take the hand of that young girl, helping her from the bench. He had watched with cold zeal as the two disappeared from the public space, into whatever private world such people disappear to, unmarked by architecture. Ariel saw the crippled figure limp in pathetic empathy with the sweet girl, saw Cosimo's vile body stain the tableau in which that young figure burned, her own body the focus of all perspective; he was a crime against reason.

The calculus of obsession echoes in its hellish multiplication those charts that illustrate the exploding population of rodents; obsession breeds ratlike and transfers from thought to thought like the plague, flowers and even in its dying flowers over and over again, crawling from itself like maggots from its own corpse; Ariel Price was lost.

He is vile. He is vile. His whole being is an affront to everything I have worked my entire life to establish: order, clarity, proportion, beauty. He is the crippled negation of man. Beast, disfigure, unground. It cannot be, and yet I saw it—and these eyes are precise—she took his repulsive hand, let him lead her from the square. They went off. Together.

The breeding of thought continues, each recursion more grotesque than the last, until Ariel's cycling mind grows into a cavern, inhabited with twisting images beside which Cosimo's form is nothing, a mere aberration in the noisome presence of the relentless grotesque. From their origin in the act of seeing, thoughts dance down the chain of being to fornicate evilly on the fecal floor of Price's caged soul.

He sees, and more than sees, the two combine in lascivious acts, choreographed obscene, entering and reentering each other, clothes wet and torn; he sees this. The great imagination, capable of visiting hell on living cities, builds a febrile sexual dance between Cosimo and Bethany, a mongrel coupling wild with canine crying and slick flesh.

"Cosimo. Mr. Neri." Ariel turned to the bent apprentice and smiled the semblance of a smile. "I want you to detail this. It is a task for you."

With a deft gesture, Ariel Price circled an area of the plan: the very center of the mall, equidistant in every direction from natural light. Ariel had plans for this space. And crucial to his plans was that the darkest room be designed by Cosimo Neri. Let him discover later what it is that he has made.

Far away from this, in the way that one story is worlds removed from another, Izzy Darlow also courts punishment. He knows better. A stranger has come to him for shelter. There are rules governing hospitality, and Izzy knows, now as well as anyone in those ruined cities, the consequences if they are broken.

But Izzy Darlow has found that the presence of this woman, even though he does not know her, has clouded his judgment. His voice is thickening in his throat; his breath too swift and audible; he finds himself staring at her when he believes her to be looking away. None of us is willing to grant this in another, however: the possibility that they too see peripherally, see more than we want them to see. Arianna sits on the floor, and she stares at the floor as she speaks to him. She knows that she is being examined. She is pleased, but disturbed.

"My father works for some of the world's most powerful men. They believe he works for them, that is; in his own mind they are his minions."

She pulls a sheaf of tattered papers out of her pocket. "These are some of his drawings. They're amazing. Look: here is where he believes he has an idea for a whole new city: a few lines of pencil, and he thinks he can redirect lives. And here: here he thinks he has perfected the house. This is a house he will want me to live in, soon, a house that he hopes will perfect me. I am an ordinary citizen, you see, in the eyes of my father. A test case. That's what I'm good for. Look at these horrible lines . . ."

Izzy gently pushes Arianna's sheaf of paper aside. She raises her eyes, questioning.

"Can we not talk for a moment?"

"Okay . . . why?" Arianna would rather talk.

Izzy kneels forward until he can feel her breath.

Arianna wants to object: "I—"

"No. Let's not talk for a moment."

This close to her, he cannot distinguish between the real and the false. Her presence envelopes him. He feels part of himself tearing away to travel a vertiginous path, the mysterious road toward union. She breathes. He tries to capture it: the regularity of her breath, the insubstantial fact of it, mere air scented with life, but it escapes him. You cannot have this moment, Izzy Darlow. It is not yours to own.

He touches her neck, and she shivers, pulls away.

"You won't let me kiss you?"

"I'm sorry. You're scaring me."

Arianna runs both hands, nervously, through her bright hair, pulling it back behind her ears only to have it fall forward again, pulling it back, breathing.

"Okay. Kiss me if you want."

Izzy clutches her, one hand on her quivering spine, one at her neck, and places his mouth on hers, which is open, pulling her breath into him and praying.

Arianna, it is not fair that anyone should suffer love like this. You will destroy me. How foolish, she thinks. We have known each other less than an hour.

She lies almost passive against his arm, eyes open, examining him: so this is what a man looks like, obsessed.

Scilla took in nothing of the mall around her: as always, she preferred to be taken in. Which she was. The secretaries, the shopkeepers, the financial analysts, all regarded Scilla with the concerned stupefaction that comfortable people reserve for alien species. She might have been a peacock, or a tapir, or a baby orangutan, so egregiously out of place did she seem in that corridor. Even the way in which she strode through the underground mall, her breath too deep and luxurious for that filtered air, her eyes too bright for that subdued illumination, contributed to this overarching sense: that she did not belong here.

Most were reconciled to the fact that creatures like Scilla cohabited, shared the vast city of Toronto with them, but most found comfort in the notion—now flaunted, and, in a way, refuted—that Scilla and her kind kept to their own domain. It was an ancient thing, good to preserve, like the medieval distinction between beast and town.

Perhaps most galling about her casual intrusion into their underground domain was how she seemed, quite falsely, to assume that she was the more sophisticated species, that she was—if we must use Darwinian metaphors—higher up on the food chain. I eat people like you, said her easy, accomplished gait, when I'm not even hungry. Between meals.

And her insistence upon walking this way—though, the truth be told, she wasn't really welcome here, despite its putative status as a public space—was sufficient in itself to alter the way they walked. Bankers, usually confident, as they occupied the highest position in this quite special geographical niche, walked quite stiffly upon witnessing Scilla: they walked with a degree of self-consciousness that did not suit them at all. Others were supposed to be conscious of them; this was the norm; it would not do to have them conscious of themselves. That was what secretaries were for.

Tom Sorrow came striding down the corridor, toward proud Scilla, yet even after seeing her his stride was undiminished. He blew her a kiss in passing.

Scilla stopped, amused. Who was this cheerful fool, so unaware of the order of things that he found her simply pleasant?

"Excuse me . . ."

Tom turned, smiling.

"I came down here for a cheap coffee. But since you're paying, I'll have something nice."

Soon they sat opposite each other over a table of bright plastic. "This mall repels me," said Scilla, staring with deep amusement into Tom's eyes. "It disgusts me. Does it disgust you?"

"I'm not easily disgusted . . ."

"I can see that. Life's just a garden of roses, isn't it. I can see you've never had a thorn in a tender place . . ."

Tom smiled. "Well, of course, you're entitled to your views, but I have to tell you, there are all sorts of clients out there who would be thrilled to rent space in a building plugged into this mall. I see the underground mall as a distinct selling feature—a very positive selling feature—of the tower itself."

Scilla once again assessed her luncheon mate. Her face radiated pity. "Do you."

"But then, this is my first week on the job, and I guess I'm still full of the excitement, you know: you might say I'm a bit of an innocent."

"Might you." Scilla was silent for a moment. "Approximately how much of this tower is empty, as we speak?"

"Well, I can't say for sure: I'm only responsible for certain floors. But I'd guess occupancy to be pretty low. At least half the floors probably have no tenants."

"Really." Scilla sat, lowering her black lips to the tips of her fingers, so that she seemed almost to be praying. All that empty space, thought Scilla. Think of it.

And the space wove about her, as black as earth: infinite tangles of burrowing space, stretching tunnels of darkness sick with buried air, and positioned in the center like a pin through the web of nerves and rising above them chilly with light: the dreadful monotony of tower.

Illumination made the underground web almost habitable, now, but in its very structure was, eternally, the strong possibility of night.

All cities have these places, and once they were charged with explicit meaning: they were the highways of the dead, the other map that echoed and mocked the street map of the living, the deep shadow cast by civic light, and the end point of human planning.

Nothing can be cast away. And every attempt to remove from view the aspects of the city that turn human will to sickness, simply creates another domain, a place beneath the light, equally complex and willful and real as the city above, but charged with exile. Here terrible things find new strength in resentment.

Scilla, sitting motionless, began to feel the history of this; she sensed in a way completely new her place in the map. And she quivered, in her contemplation, with this new awareness: of the space that made her into the spider, the being at the center, the mistress of the web.

Perhaps the mall was not without possibility, after all.

Izzy clutches Arianna, and she remains in his arms, amused. It does not seem to matter if he kisses her. She examines the facts of his room: all of the books, scattered on the desk and floor, the notes to himself, taped to the walls, the disorder. This is the confusion in which he lives.

The sink is clear of dishes; she imagines that he does not know how to cook. No flowers, no pets, nothing living in this cold apartment. She wonders whether he knows how to share space with another living thing.

Izzy slides a hand up and beneath her dress, reaching for contact that has not been offered, and Arianna pulls away, eyes smoldering.

He stammers, "I'm sorry."

"You're sorry."

Izzy, blood in his cheeks, cannot meet her stare.

"What would you do if the angel arrived at your door in disguise, and begged a room for the night?"

Izzy does not understand; he understands little in his current state; he reaches for her again.

"What would you do?"

"I don't know. I'm not sure what you're asking me . . ."

"I'm asking you how you would behave if you were put to the test. If it were your gate the visitor graced, if it were you weighed in the balance."

"I . . . I don't know what I'd do . . ."

"You'd try to fuck her, Izzy Darlow. That's what you would do. You'd try to fuck her."

As Scilla and her new friend emerged from the corporate gloom into the gray light of King Street, a man lurching down the sidewalk fell to the pavement in front of them. His head met the concrete with a breaking sound, and he bled from the side of his mouth. His eyes, open, focused on nothing. Unwittingly, Tom Sorrow grasped the arm of the woman he had just met. Scilla did not move.

The crowd flowing down the street parted for the fallen man, as water divides around a stone in the river, but no one stopped.

"We should do something." Tom said this, but he made no motion to approach the bleeding man. "I think he's dead."

A circle of young men, dressed in filthy clothes, sat on the pavement some feet away. One of them spoke in a quiet voice, and the others smoked and listened. One of the listeners may have been a woman, but she was dressed the same way as the men, and her face was obscured by hair.

As Tom and Scilla stood frozen on the sidewalk, the leader of this circle, still speaking quietly, raised himself from his haunches and approached the corpse. His followers fell in behind him.

"We saw him fall," said Tom. "I think . . . I think he hit his head pretty badly. I think he may be dead."

The leader lifted his eyes and looked into Tom's. "He is dead."

Tom's grip on Scilla's arm tightened, as the leader knelt in his torn clothes and closed the dead man's eyes. Again, the stranger lifted his head and stared at Tom Sorrow. "Do you believe in death?"

Tom did not know what to say. How could one not believe in death? He pulled on Scilla's arm: "Let's go. Let's get out of here."

"No." For reasons she did not understand, Scilla wanted to stay. Why would anyone not believe in death?

The followers waited patiently behind the leader, as he cradled the bleeding head. Tom's hand on Scilla's arm trembled. "We have to leave . . ."

"One moment . . ."

The leader smiled, an infinitely sad smile. "Yes. One moment is all." He leaned forward and placed his lips against the dead man's ear, whispering words that no one could make out. He seemed to speak for a long time, but Scilla, thinking back, could not be sure: perhaps it was only a single word. Tom shivering.

A policeman sauntered over. "What's happening here? Come on: off the sidewalk." He moved the dead man's leg, rudely, with the edge of his boot. The leader held up a hand: wait.

"Is he sick? What's going on here?"

"No. Not sick. He is sleeping. One moment."

The dead man's eyes opened, terrified, and he wiped the blood from his mouth. The leader smiled. As the policeman evaluated the scene, suspiciously, Tom Sorrow pulled Scilla away into the anonymity of King Street.

PART THREE: ELEVATION

Further, Augustine tells us, before the Fall, Adam had been capable of moving his sexual member with as much control as a fallen man might exercise over a finger, arm or foot. But now, infected by the stain of original sin, the sexual organs functioned with no regard to their owner, in retribution for their sin of disobedience.

—SUSAN HASKINS, *MARY MAGDALEN*

A BRIEF HISTORY OF DARKNESS

The labyrinth is an image of the city. And the city itself is an image of the human mind; Anthony Velvel has explored this at perverse length in Lethe Remembered. *The labyrinth, then, is a meta-metaphor. An image of an image of an image. The mind is always looking to expand its hegemony: this is the drive toward architecture. After torturing its own substance into a semblance of submission, through the device of reason (the rational will is a thumbscrew; it makes the booming, buzzing confusion say "this coheres," despite the inclination toward chaos), the mind turns outward; and the natural sphere of colonization is the realm apprehended immediately in front of the bright, acquisitive eyes: the domain of the real.*

In forcing the real to conform to rules—in building cities—the mind naturally chooses a familiar form. The city takes, inevitably, the shape of the mind itself.

But the mind does not know its own shape. And the part of the soul that is illegible, even to the peering, insolent ego, finds its way into the real by a process of duplication: the city breeds another city, gloomy and infernal and unknown to the light, a dark mirror.

As Velvel makes so abundantly clear in his study, this sub-city is a place of meaning and exile: it is where the citizens of daylight banish their shame.

When the queen fornicates with the bull from the sea and gives birth to a monster, the king—whose own arrogance moved him to keep the sacred bull that was not his—decides to banish the loathsome offspring to a place beneath the city, a bleak place that looks for all the world like a grid of streets, except that there is no map and only one exit.

And the architect—whose arrogance moved him to create the device whereby the queen violated nature and took the great bull between her white legs—turns his genius toward the creation of the labyrinth.

When Ariel Price finds that the city of Toronto offers no place for the proper expansion of his lust toward the dancing girl, he proposes to build an underground mall. And when the girl dies, the mall becomes the type of itself: the sub-city, the sewer, the catacomb . . . the grave.

Tom waited nervously in the space between the towers, a space made somehow even less hospitable at night by the blindness of the curtain walls. At night, there was no pretense of human intent. The landscape became purely what it was: a funereal sculpture, tall as death.

Tom busied himself by imagining the occupants of the various floors. The fifteenth was now home to secretive Armenian developers; Tom himself had closed the deal, but he had never met his clients, nor it seemed had any of their employees. Still, something serious was being pursued on the fifteenth floor these days; legions of smartly suited peons, burning with Masonic fire, would file into the myriad elevators and press the glowing 15.

Seventeen was divided between two law offices. Lists of names, one list entirely Jewish, the other entirely not. Tom had leased to the Jewish firm and had been instrumental in calming the concerns of the other. Now the two firms cohabited politely, if they had never precisely managed to bridge their theological divide. True, thought Tom, the difference between your personal savior and merely one in a line of pretentious false messiahs is a big difference in interpretation.

Where was that woman? The night was oppressive. Sometimes the humidity in this city was impossible, a thickness of atmosphere that made it all but impossible to concentrate. At night the wet would generally lift, but tonight an invisible heaviness hung in the sky, and the stars disappeared from the human sphere. Tom would have preferred greatly to be in bed, but this woman was intriguing.

No, Tom was not one to pass up an opening. Tom Sorrow was a closer. "You don't get the sale you don't ask for." Just one of the little maxims that made coherent driving sense of his life.

This Scilla was difficult, perhaps, but no more difficult than the most obstinate client. And she had phoned. She had phoned him. Yes, the pretext was an interest in the tower, but Tom knew otherwise. This woman was not interested in the Letztesmann Tower; this woman was interested in him. Their experience on King Street had bound them together; he was sure of it. For a few days he had found the memory of the fallen man unsettling, but now it remained in his mind simply as this: the event that bound him to the strange and lovely woman.

Odd that she had requested they meet at midnight. But women always wanted something unique in their targeted man, and what did he, Tom, have that was more indisputably unique than unfettered access to the Letztesmann Tower, at any hour of the day or night?

Fine, Miss Scilla. You want a little tour of the tower at midnight, it can be arranged.

A warm stagnant wind blew up from the grating beneath him, and Tom gagged briefly: it was a premonition, not so much a scent or a sensation against the skin; it was a nauseous wave of intuition that swept over his innocent mind like the remembrance of an ancient atrocity, a sickness of flesh and memory. Christ, what is in the air tonight?

A young girl danced in the square in front of Tom, where a moment before there had been no one.

"Hello?"

It was not Scilla, but a young girl, perhaps fourteen. She did not hear him. She danced, and Tom approached. The sickness grew in his mind, tempered by a peculiar strain of pity. Or not so much pity as sadness, a mourning urge directed toward something unknown, something young and decayed.

The girl danced strangely, as if she were in pain. And as Tom approached, he saw that one of her feet was barely a foot: it was crushed flesh, pulped and bleeding, and the girl danced on it. Tom turned away, and staring unfocused at the broad white paving stones emptied his stomach.

"You unhappy, sailor?"

Scilla stood against a glass wall, one hand on her hip, her mouth turned up in an expression of wry contempt.

"I . . . oh god . . ."

Without turning around, Tom wiped at his mouth and gestured at the place where the young girl was dancing.

"Yes?"

Scilla's cold smile did not fade, and she was looking precisely at the young bleeding girl.

Steeling himself, Tom glanced back there as well. The girl

was gone. How could this be? With her horribly maimed foot, how could she have found her way out of the public space so quickly? The sickness subsided as quickly as it had risen, and Tom stood upright.

"I . . . god, I thought I saw something . . ."

"Caught a fright, big boy? Past your bedtime?"

"I must have eaten something."

"Yes, I can see that."

Scilla thought deeply about the mall as she lay the blade against her arm. Lay it there, shining, a jewel of sharpness, all potency and new. Razor blades always had that for her: an almost mystical perfection. So thin that they slid between other things, even if there was no opening, so thin and sharp that they opened a path. Objects had qualities, for Scilla, and sharpness was a quality that she especially admired. The sharp edge was subtle, almost imperceptible, a whisper that drew blood.

She lay the blade against her arm. When she flexed her thin muscle, the blade moved and shone. The mall was indeed an interesting place. Deep, as places go. A tall building with blind windows that mirror the city, and beneath it a vast underground mall that mirrors the city: if you hold a mirror to a mirror you get infinity.

She caught her face made grotesque in the rectangular blade, which now drew blood. Scilla never felt pain at moments like this. She simply felt something, whereas, if she did not cut herself, she felt nothing. Sharpness gives feeling. Just a little blood, for today, and another scar to match the many: scars that indicated like a diary moments when Scilla had felt something.

Her partner Campbell had shown her a place where, at the

moment of the moon's full light, a manhole cover would appear in the blank pavement. He had lectured her, in that way of his that was so abstract yet entertaining—a tiny professor with jagged hair—he had said this to her: "Someday you will want to enter the street beneath the street, and this is the way in. Remember where it is. Someday you will have an idea of the place below, the place of confrontation, and you will want ingress. I am telling you: this is the way in."

And the manhole had shimmered for a moment, like the water that forms in the distance even on the driest road, then disappeared.

Scilla remembered that spot, and though she had not seen Campbell in years, she made her way now to the place where he had stood at midnight to show her the entrance. The blood was drying on her arm, and she paid it no mind.

The fool Tom Sorrow had not been able to show her anything of interest, but he might still prove useful. Scilla wanted access to parts of the tower as yet unknown to Sorrow, despite his official position. It was a question of perspective: he would have to learn much before such aspects revealed themselves. Scilla, on the other hand, could stare briefly at any place and know whether it contained mystery.

She stood in the middle of Shuter Street, alone, and stared at the blank pavement. No cars. The surface shone with the tar of the full moon. Nothing. Certainly this was where Campbell had stood, lecturing; this was where the steel cover had emerged, a round plate of metal stamped with a pattern of squares like a chess board; but nothing. Somebody began to sing.

Scilla looked up, but the voice seemed to come from the air. She closed her eyes and focused on the place of the sound, and began to make tentative steps toward it. The voice grew stronger.

He was there curled like a monkey into the corner between two walls, his arms about his knees, his eyes pale blue and a deep gash on his forehead. He looked straight up at her and sang in a clear boy soprano.

As with Campbell, Scilla had the sense that this boy was not entirely flesh, not flesh like hers that she could cut. Unlike Campbell, this boy seemed good. Nervous, Scilla followed him as he stood and stepped out into the silence of the moon.

So I suppose I should tell you a bit about me. I've been alone for a long time. I died in a car that was burning, and I lost my family—or rather, they lost me. But for some reason I was not permitted to leave. My grandfather left—Abba—he left in the fire, but I was made to stay. It's hard to say what my time is like, now. I walk. I walk, and I sing, and I try to put together the pieces of the story, which seem sometimes overwhelming in their separateness and pain.

I died in the city of Toronto. And I died because of what that city did to my family. There was something terrible at the heart of that city, written into it like a code beneath the skin, and it hurt my family deeply, broke it like an egg, and left me on the other side of the fire, still here but not really here, no longer a citizen. I wanted to find out what it was; what it was about Toronto that had done this to me.

I had a sense that it was the man, whoever it was, who had made the city tall. It was his fault.

I have had some years now to think about this, and for much of that time I have stood facing a black tower. You can't see me. I have stood between secretaries, and bankers having lunch, and stared up at the black tower, which seemed from the start—and only now do I begin to understand this—the emblem, the symbol, you might even say the handwriting, of this man. The man I had to find.

I say that you can't see me. That's not entirely true. When I sing, I open eyes that are already open, so that they see just a little beyond sight. And then they see me. So, if I want you to see me, I sing.

I wanted this woman, the one with the fresh blood on her arm, to see me. She seemed part of the larger picture. I knew this: that she was thinking about the mall beneath the black tower, and that this was part of what I thought about. And I knew that she had once known Campbell, my brother's friend.

My brother is part of the family that is lost. Izzy. He was unhappy, and then he met a boy named Campbell, who made him see himself for what he was—unhappy—and it ruined him. But this is another story, for another time. Anyway, Campbell is a bit like me: sometimes you don't see him.

This woman, the one with the scars, had come to the place in the road where the opening appears. I can't tell you why, but we all know this—Campbell, myself, the others—we know about the places that open to let the living look briefly upon the cities beneath the earth. It's an old business; I don't quite understand it. But the dead and the living meet, when they do, which is rare, at the places that open.

This woman was at the wrong place. The road here was not going to open, on this night—I knew this, and I can't really say how—and besides, it was never going to open into the mall. I knew the place that opened into the mall. I had been there.

Scilla followed the boy, the sign on his forehead the sign on her arm. The song that he sang made her think in a hazy manner of a story that existed outside of her: a book that she hadn't read. This story had a beginning, middle and end; it had people that mattered, and these people suffered through real lives; and yet she had never met them and did not know their story. Life seemed infinitely richer, listening to the young boy's song. He said: There is meaning. There is. It lives in a place. You simply haven't been there.

The song made her long for this place.

She tried to talk to him. "Do you have a name, kid?"

He stopped singing when she spoke, and it was almost unbearable: as if the lid had been taken off the vacuum, and frigid air full of death rushed in to fill the void. He didn't say anything. "No," she said. "Forget it. Keep singing."

They did not go far. It was a tangled route—again, hinting at meaning: as if the map of the route they took referred to a deeper map, which referred in turn to a place—but it did not take them far from Shuter Street. It took them to a tiny windswept plaza: the Letztesmann Plaza. A space between the towers.

Scilla stood facing the boy, and between them lay a steel grating, a square grid choked with leaves. The leaves themselves, though dead and misshapen, had streaks of alien color; they looked to have fallen from trees far from the plaza.

Scilla lifted one of the leaves with the tip of her finger; it clung there, wet, and she examined it. A vein of deep red divided the leaf, and from this central vein tributaries broke off and branched. She rolled the wet leaf into a ball and flicked it away.

The boy sang.

The square grating moved.

Scilla was not frightened—she was rarely frightened—but transfixed, as the grating screeched briefly, old rusted surfaces grinding against stone, and sank into the plaza as if it had merely floated there for years, like wood on water, and was now too heavy.

It left in its place a square hole.

Scilla knelt to stare into the hole: a rusted ladder was bolted to the side and descended into shadow. When she looked up, the boy was gone, though his voice seemed to linger in the air, barely audible, coloring the wind. She pushed the black hair from her face with a willful gesture and tested the top rung.

It seemed solid. As solid as anything on this night that seemed to defy structure. And so, letting herself down, gingerly, into the narrow shaft, she grasped the cold ladder, felt with her feet in the darkness, and began to descend.

The square of sky receded above her, growing smaller and more dim until it seemed an illusion, a trick of the darkness itself: an attempt by the eye to put an object in the void. Perhaps it was no longer there at all, the opening. It hardly mattered. What was real now was the ladder, the bones in her hands, and the careful searching movement of her feet as she found her way down.

Astonishing, the depth of the shaft. Scilla felt herself climb past layers of shadow, whole cities and strata of nature, piercing history itself. And now she could see.

It was a gradual thing, the return of the light. For the longest time this too seemed an illusion: dancing specks of light, amoe-balike in the darkness—when Scilla closed her eyes these danc-ing particles would always appear, a kind of visual dreaming—but these particles began to pull together now and take form. And besides: her eyes were open. She was seeing something.

The light was whitish and unreal, flickering. Scilla narrowed her eyes, but there was nothing yet to focus on: just a faint glow of something, stale and subterranean, and the ladder at her face when she turned back. But she could see, and was descending toward sight; that was something.

Her feet met steel.

She looked down, at the grating beneath her feet, through which the pale light illuminated her legs. There was a small space to stand beside the grate, and from there she could kneel and peer through the grid.

A young girl stood well below her, staring up at the grating. Their eyes met. Scilla pulled at the steel with her fingers, and it came away in her hands. She descended to meet the girl, who stepped backward to make way.

The young girl looked up and beyond Scilla, to the boy standing above her, and for a moment her eyes glowed with a light of recognition, and then they returned to their state: in-ward and strange. Scilla glanced back too, but the boy was gone.

"Priscilla?" The girl's voice came out of somewhere distant, as if down through time. "Priscilla."

"I call myself Scilla. But yeah, that's my name."

The young girl turned, on her good foot, and it was only then that Scilla noticed the girl was lame: her other foot was crushed and bloody, although she walked on it as if it were whole. And also strange in the way she walked was how her feet seemed to meet an invisible floor suspended above the floor that Scilla could see. The girl took tiny trancelike steps forward into the darkened mall, and Scilla hurried after.

"What's your name?"

The girl stopped and looked at Scilla, said nothing, then continued to step forward.

"I've been calling myself Scilla for years. Only my mother ever calls me Priscilla, and I haven't seen her since I was fourteen. How did you know my name?"

The girl moved forward on her floor that was some inches above the hard floor beneath Scilla's feet. She said nothing.

What are we to make of Ariel Price? This, dear reader, depends upon which are the threads we choose to unravel. A man of genius—even a man of Price's caliber—is woven of many strands, and our understanding of that man will depend upon which clew we choose to follow, and where it leads us.

Others have seen Price as a braid of three bright paths of thought winding down from the nineteenth century. Axial symmetry. Reason. And responsibility. Others have not looked very closely.

Yes, you find symmetry in Price, as you do in every creation of every man and every animal, down from the beginning of time. And the rational approach to construction is, quite simply, a feature of even the most ornamentally obscene architecture, until very recently. Social responsibility? Please. It is a feature of the idolater that he must project goodness into the beast. Ariel Price cared no more for the occupants of his building than does a chef for the pieces of meat that he throws in a stew.

And yet there is one bright thread discernible, if you look closely, in the tangle that is the Price soul. I may be the first properly to have noticed this clew, this clue—pardon me, dear reader—but I have followed it for some years, now, and it has taken me to the center of a complex place. A very complex place.

The thread is the color of Arrogance, and the Will to Dominate. Follow me, if you dare, and I shall lead you into the murderous place, into the full bleak night of the architect's being.

It is no coincidence that the final Price masterpiece features, so prominently, a tombstone growing from the heart of a labyrinth.

Theseus Crouch writes these last words, "a tombstone growing from the heart of a labyrinth," with deft, vain strokes, in turquoise ink. Yes. Beautifully put. And some readers might take issue with his pun on the word "clew," but he knows, Theseus knows, that the greatest poets are sometimes given to the most execrable puns. Shakespeare, he imagines, would have been no more welcome at a party than he is.

The competition has received his fax. A fax machine lets you know this: that your message has been received. Some fool in the Sinai Desert imagines himself to be constructing a life of Price, but Theseus Crouch feels certain that he has frightened him off. And even if he does not succeed in shaking this irritant, Crouch knows that there is precious little chance the competing scholar has found out what he, Crouch, has uncovered in the foundations of the Letztesmann Tower. What is this fool doing in the desert? Price never contributed to a single design in the Middle East. In fact, Price's views concerning the Jewish people

123

have long been suspect, and will, after the publication of the Crouch biography, be common knowledge.

And Ariel Price himself will, by now, have read the first chapter, which Theseus Crouch sent to the architect's apartment in Paris. He will know, by now, that he is being hunted down, cornered and identified, rendered transparent and placed on display. You have positioned us in glass towers, Herr Price, and I shall place you in a glass cabinet, like an insect. For the longest time you promised us that glass would permit us a perspicuous view, a panoptical view, but now it is clear to all but the densest modernist: glass is a traitor. You can look out, yes, but we can look in.

It had not been easy finding the Price address; the great architect was living in a modest apartment a block from the Marais, in an Arab district. The Price bankruptcy had been widely publicized—he had been sued by his employees for unpaid wages, and it had ruined the practice—but few people knew where the great man had retired. A suite had been constructed on the top floor of the Letztesmann Tower, but Crouch has investigated that thoroughly: it has remained empty, all these years. No, Price is in Paris, living a modest life, licking his wounds, and watching with satisfaction as his reputation blossoms long after he has ceased to build. The lawsuit was a blemish, quickly forgiven by a public accustomed to unusual behavior from genius. These days, it is Price's place in history that is focused upon, mostly. He is settling nicely into the canon. In truth, his position is so apparently fixed among the immortals that one silly critic has referred to the Letztesmann Tower as "Price's posthumous masterpiece." The man has achieved such a degree of perfection in his reputation that he might as well be dead.

Theseus Crouch imagines the great man, satisfied with himself in his tiny apartment in Paris. Never mind that he has never achieved material success, personally: he has changed the shape of the city forever; and what is this apart from the greatest material success? Price has molded the shape of matter, altered the architectonic instinct of the species; human worker bees will be fashioning the hive in Price-like ways for centuries to come.

Price, for all his faults, has never been avaricious. His greed is purely metaphysical.

Theseus Crouch plans to take away from him the only thing that ever mattered to the voracious architect: his place in history.

Izzy and Arianna have sat together in awkward conversation since his aborted attempt to seduce her. His face is burning, but what he feels is not shame. He is desperate to find a way through to her again; minutes ago they were almost close; she let him kiss her.

"Are you hungry, Arianna?"

"I don't have any money."

"I'll buy you dinner."

She says nothing, picks at the nail polish that is fragmenting on her fingernail.

"Let me buy you dinner."

Arianna smiles: an excited, warm smile, unexpected. "Okay. Okay, I'll let you buy me dinner."

They descend in silence, and turn toward the long row of mysterious truck bays, where snub-nosed delivery trucks, chocolate-colored trucks with gold lettering, idle and imbibe matter from complex steel veins. All night the trucks come and go, lending a false sense of community to the desolate neighborhood. Izzy takes her to the Bar.

The Bar has no name: it has always been called this. And now it has survived for so long in the collective consciousness of the city that the civic elders have decreed that the neon sign cannot be altered—it is a piece of memory, all that remains of dockworkers and whores from when this was one of the world's great ports—and it will always be called the Bar.

The bartender stands beneath a dusty collection of alchemical glass: impossible bottles, turned in on their own stomachs, bottles that contain themselves and the occasional ghost. He nods at Izzy, but the waitresses are not happy that he is here. He comes here most nights, usually alone and uncommunicative, but sometimes with a woman. The waitresses have seen Izzy with a woman before; they know that the meal is as likely as not to end in tears and recrimination; they have had to ask him to leave more than once.

Izzy likes the waitresses here; they are mostly English and Irish, and cheerful in the strong, determined way that bar workers have generally been in hard cities. He knows that one of them makes marionettes, idiosyncratic puppets, erotic—she told him about them once, but she no longer speaks to him. Izzy has been here too many times in no mood to speak, or with some woman bent on public grief.

For a time the Bar was a brothel, when alcohol was prohibited by law, and the ghosts of that period are the most gregarious. Izzy has sat with syphilitic girls, gray and translucent, who interrupt dinner with barely whispered stories of small coastal towns, eloquent sailors, promises and rape. On some nights the dead madam howls so insistently that she can be heard above the electric guitars.

It is even rumored that the playwright used to come here, that it is here that he drank with the Iceman.

Arianna and Izzy sit, led to their table by an unsmiling waitress, and the loudness of the Bar swallows them like the night. Arianna is happy here, no longer accusatory; she turns out to be one of those good people who cannot remain unaffected by the happiness of others; she even moves her arms seductively as if dancing to the music. It is true that Izzy also finds pleasure in the happiness of others—Arianna now is lifting him to another place—so perhaps he is not all bad.

They drink tall fat glasses of Irish ale. Arianna small behind hers. The food is ordinary, unevolved from centuries of ordinary bar food, overcooked, dripping with fat, satisfying. Arianna is changed; she flashes her eyes, bites her lower lip, and nods her head to the slow guitar.

With Arianna capricious and happy, swaying with bright eyes to the music, Izzy feels that anything might be possible. The most foolish and pervasive force in human life—as if we are not structured with our eyes fixed forward upon death—is hope, and yet. And yet. Arianna dances with her arms, eyes glittering; she laughs.

A translucent girl with a sore on her lip has drifted into the chair beside her. The girl scratches a hole in the paper covering the table, and begins to weep. Arianna does not see her. Perhaps nobody sees the sick girl, barely dressed, except Izzy; perhaps this has nothing to do with sight.

And the music stops.

With a small gesture, the bartender has restored silence: a

band is setting up instruments at the front of the Bar, and the stereo has been switched off to give them the opportunity to tune their instruments.

The change is instantaneous. Izzy can see it in Arianna's eyes, the set of her mouth: nothing is any good any more. Happiness gone with a gesture, off like a switch.

"I live with my father."

"You . . . told me."

"Yes."

"So? So what's your father like?"

"What's he like?" Arianna laughs, a sound without joy. "Very brilliant. They all are, aren't they. Fathers, architects. So very brilliant. I wish they'd turn the music back on . . ."

Izzy waits. Perhaps now he will know why this woman has chosen to interrupt his life.

"The wonderful things my father made. Devices. Fountains, fantastical devices, all manner of invention, so that our lives might be improved. He insists that I live with them: his toys. He made me a pair of wings, once, hoping that I would test them for him, fly for him, but I refused. I told him that I did not want an airplane. I did not want a boat. I wanted a home, Father, a home. He hasn't spoken to me much since . . ."

Arianna continues to speak, but it is as if the gray girl has infected her soul: Arianna's voice rises, and her words pull apart.

"I was made to eat his master plan, every night, mixed with pieces of steel and glass. He tore down my house while I was sleeping, every night, and remade it, so that I might be happy. Remade it with terrible devices, hooks and collars, made my lovely house into a machine. And I am supposed to live there."

Arianna is speaking loudly now, angrily, with an edge of hysteria to her voice. The couple at the table next to us, disturbed, has requested the bill. The waitress—the lovely one who carves marionettes—is glaring at me with contempt.

Arianna lifts her fork and drags it, viciously, against the skin of her arm, the tines leaving four red marks. A race to the grave.

"Arianna, please don't . . ." but Izzy is too late; before he can grasp her hand she has pushed the steel points beneath her skin. She laughs viciously; Izzy can tell that she feels no pain.

"You don't know what it's like to be naked for my father. Sometimes I just wanted to grow hair, everywhere, grow a pelt like a dog so he wouldn't be able to see me. You think I don't know how your mind works. Boy. Architect."

The waitress brings the check to the table beside ours, and—unbidden—delivers ours as well. Arianna turns to her. "I'm not ready to pay."

Holding her hands up, the waitress retreats. The milky girl, light pouring through her like smoke, scratches the back of her hands until they bleed. She begins to sing an ancient, obscene ditty.

Arianna has focused again on Izzy Darlow with burning eyes. "You're evil. You don't know it, but you are. You have nothing good in you, nothing sweet, nothing kind . . ." She begins to cry. "Nothing but huge, horrible ideas, things you want to make me into, horrible plans. I just wanted a place to stay. That's all I ever wanted from my father, was a place to stay. Maybe I don't want to be part of your story, Izzy Darlow. Maybe I hate you."

Izzy touches her arm, where she has punctured the skin. She pulls back, too quickly: she recoils as if from something terrifying, monstrous. The fear in her eyes—eyes that seem to be looking at him, but god knows what they see—cuts him like judgment.

The bartender is walking their way with a determined look. Izzy fumbles for his wallet. He will leave a huge amount of money, more than he can afford. "No, no change . . ."

Izzy stands, but Arianna won't let him near her. Knocking over her chair, she forces her way through the crowd milling about the exit.

Izzy Darlow follows, his eyes averted. They watch him leave—he knows that he is being watched—but he stares at the floor.

Arianna is crouched by a fire hydrant, rocking. Izzy does not know this woman, and she is violent, but still he wants to say: Ari, let me give you my world; it at least is calm; I'll take this from you and bear it for a while.

The architect Price rises miraculously from his encounter with damnation, rises miraculously in a green bus through the greener drenched landscape of Galilee, rises like an apparition (except that he himself is the victim of apparitions, is Ariel Price) into the mountainous region containing the most mysterious of the holy cities, the city of exile within the nation, the center of mystical reasoning and the teaching of the Great Lion: Tzvat. Or Safad. Or Zefat. No matter, that this city cannot properly lay claim to a singular appellation: it is the city in which names are more than names, in which names have the power to open the locked interior of things. The city as key. And Ariel Price, less than any man—and this was a city distant to the mental workings of most—has the key to this city.

He knows that Tzvat is considered the font of secret lore. That here, in an astonishingly brief period, the great Kabbalist established the core and canon of Jewish mystical teaching. Ariel Price is not without regard for the secrets of the Jews. Truth be told, in his suspicious mind he has greatly magnified the power of this closely guarded doctrine: hatred bloats the enemy, and no matter how hard he has tried to dismiss the pesky race as vulgar, striving, and coarse, he has never managed to shake a growing suspicion that they guard a hidden realm of knowledge that even Wagner would have envied and sought, had he known of it.

And it is here, in desperate flight from his own secret, that Ariel Price comes to discern the healing secret of the Other. On the top of a mountain he finds Tzvat, fully medieval. Winding streets and climbing walls, tiny cavelike synagogues with painted columns, blue and purple and gold. A celebration of smallness, of the potency of the microscopic, a model in miniature of great Jerusalem, and that much stronger in its mystery as a concentrated liquid is to a sea of diluted substance. Ariel Price is disoriented. Because Tzvat, like Jerusalem, is a monument to urban complexity, to the possibility of getting lost. A labyrinth. The city was designed to confound orientation, and in so doing to drive the human mind beyond the material sphere.

Price detests it.

Where Tel Aviv is scientific, Cartesian and positivistic in its mechanical sprawl, Tzvat is gnomic, inward, intestinal and strange, a city built by accretion like a codex with its annotation, no lines evident except that they turn in upon themselves and disappear, complexity within complexity: a repulsive city, Tzvat.

Merely walking, trying to get to a place, Ariel Price is battered by nausea. This is an urban plan?

A tiny man, wearing a Walkman and tallith, takes the bewildered Price by the arm.

"Lost?"

Price looks at the fat little man, who is bearded and idiotic with hospitality.

"You look lost, my friend. Tell me: you Jewish? Both sides? Mother and father?"

Ariel Price is inclined to dismiss the man with a sharp observation, but he suppresses the urge. This is the city of mystery, and he has come here to pry open its secret; perhaps this fool is—despite his appearance—a gatekeeper. Or a man who knows the gatekeeper.

"Yes," says Ariel Price. "I am a Jew."

The tiny man twinkles and shines. He removes the headphones from his ears, which are wound about with braid upon braid, and clasps Ariel Price by the shoulders.

"Welcome!"

Scilla follows in the warm footsteps of the crippled girl. They are warm, the places in midair that the girl has moved from, the places in the invisible floor through which Scilla wades. We are on two separate planes, thinks Scilla, but I can feel yours; your world stretches out at my feet like a sea. She follows the young girl.

In the distance the light continues to grow. As Scilla walks, she feels again a presence at her shoulder. She turns, and the young boy is there, a step behind her, his forehead bleeding.

She notes that he too seems to walk on an invisible floor some inches above her own. He points ahead, and Scilla looks back to the young girl, who steps with ritual steps into the growing but still dim light.

It hardly seems possible: they are approaching a city. Here, beneath the streets of Toronto, a vast landscape stretches out before Scilla: a skein of night-soaked streets, far more dense and tall than anything in the world above.

The boy at her shoulder begins to speak.

"You are entering the city that Toronto dreams. This is the form the city takes in its mind at night: a city of garbage, narrow and evil and tall, dark in its ways and hard to know, the dream. When I was alive in that place above us, I knew—we all knew— that there was something more, that our steps on the cold streets were echoing somewhere much vaster, a place we couldn't see but could only sense, and this is that city."

The young girl turns back to face Scilla and the boy. Her eyes are shining. She smiles. "My name is Bethany. This is my home. Welcome."

Ariel Price sits in a tiny cold room at the hostel as his host lectures him about the laws. "We have many laws. We have many of them. And yes, you have to obey them all. Over five hundred little laws, and you have to think about every one of them. Or you're going to be a bad Jew. And we don't want that, do we?" The host, a tall skinny man in black with a plaited beard, makes a "tch" noise every so often between observations. "No, we don't want that."

The little man installed Ariel in a bunk bed at the hostel

and introduced him to the host. Meals are free, but in order to receive food, Ariel is required to study every morning. This is his morning session with the host.

Ariel is confused by the man's accent. "You're not from here, are you."

The host laughs. "I'm from Brooklyn. We're all from Brooklyn. The center of the faith, you think it's Jerusalem, but you're wrong. It's here, in Tzvat, and it's in Brooklyn. That's where the center is.

"Let me tell you something. About the laws. About the center of the faith. How come we have all these laws? I'll tell you. You didn't ask me, but I'll tell you."

The host leans forward, close to the delirious Price, and whispers in his ear. "They ruined the Temple. Destroyed it. Maybe you heard about this? That's what they did. The Second Temple. And it was never rebuilt."

"I know something about this."

"Of course you do! Of course you do! You're Jewish, and how could you not know about the worst thing that ever happened to us?"

The host stops, and he closes his eyes. As he corrects himself, the color and happiness bleeds from his face: "The second worst thing."

Ariel and the host sit in uncomfortable silence for a moment. But the host brightens up. "So you know about this, how the Temple got destroyed. Now you might just think this was a material thing: so, a big synagogue gets destroyed? So what? What's the problem with this? You build another one . . ."

"I am an architect."

"So you know about this. It's easy: you build another one, right?"

"Building is not easy."

"See, you're a smart man. You're a smart one. 'Building is not easy.' I like that. And it's true. So, sometimes building, it becomes so hard that instead of doing it, you just pick up with all your friends and family, with your whole people, and you wander the face of the earth. That's what you do, instead of building, because building is so hard. But what are you going to do now? You have no Temple. The Temple, which is where you did everything—sacrifices, prayer, everything—you don't have any more. You have no home. And your God, Blessed be He, has turned His face away. Do you know this story? After the destruction of the Temple, when we all went out into the world, He turned his face away from us. He's there—of course, He's always there—but He's not looking any more. So what are you going to do?"

Ariel, mechanically, spreads his hands: I don't know. What?

"Yes! That is the question. And so we have these laws. Now you were asking, these hundreds of little laws, what do they mean? Why should I wash my hands just so? Well, I'm a simple man; I'm not a great rabbi; but the way I understand it is this."

The host plays with his long beard, makes a clucking noise, and closes his eyes.

"We have these laws because that's how we carry the Temple with us, as human beings, alone on this planet. We make a temple out of ourselves, by observing. This sounds stupid—I know this sounds stupid—but let me tell you. I wandered the desert for many years. I was a hippie—you're too old for this, but you know what a hippie is. I was searching for something. We were all searching for something. We Jews, in particular, we search. Me, I was doing acid in Sinai and waiting for the burning bush to speak to me, but I have friends who went to the ashram

135

in India, who went to Colorado and Oregon, who tried to find meaning—pardon me—between the legs of a shiksa. All of them, like me, tiny wavering flames, tiny souls, too small to light a cigarette, never mind vast enough to illuminate the great laws.

"We were homeless! That's what it was. We were without a home. And the difference between a Jew, and the other homeless people out there?" The host leaned close again, and whispered fiercely. "We need a home. We need it. That's what the Jewish soul is: it's a compass, and it always points in one direction, and that direction is home."

The host stands, and begins to stab the air with his finger, clucking the while.

"And so we Jews, we're like turtles. Until the Temple is rebuilt—and that day will come soon, sooner than you think, my friend—we carry our home with us, like turtles. We carry it with us, every day, in the shape of the laws. And that's why you want to wash your hands just so. Because otherwise, my friend, you have no roof over your head. You're a turtle without a shell. You ever see a turtle without a shell? It's a sorry sight.

"And so, you asked me about the laws, and you asked me about the center of the faith. Well, you didn't ask me, but I'm going to tell you. What's a nice boy like me doing in a mountain town in Galilee? I used to play tenor. I saw Coltrane once; I listened to Dolphy and Ornette. And now I'm here, washing my hands in a special way, and instructing lost puppies—you'll pardon me, my friend, but you are a lost puppy, and you have come here for a reason—because this is where I can observe the laws. And because of this, because of my community here, this is the center of the faith. Yes, I could go back to Brooklyn. But I feel that would be the wrong thing to do. Once you have come here, once you have done the right thing and moved to the Holy Land, you should not leave. And so I am here.

"That is the end of today's lesson. Enjoy lunch. I hope I have helped you."

You do not know what death is. I say this, knowing. I have died, and from here I can see what you do not know. We race to the grave and at the grave we bear witness and from the grave we look back and piece together what we saw during that race which was feverish and all too fast, blurred with the indistinction of life. My name is Joshua Darlow.

I would like to tell you a story.

Once upon a time, in an age undistinguished, there was a city particularly gray, and in that city lived a joyful man by the name of Tom Sorrow.

Tom, like most residents, was unaware of the city's fallen nature, because he had experienced nothing more in his brief life. He was satisfied, just as the sow is satisfied in her pen so long as she is fed and the pen remains the best of worlds known to her. Tom, however, unlike the sow, had the capacity to experience much, and to compare experiences in his mind. There was always the possibility that Tom would see something to move himself beyond the complacency of the pen. Tom, we might say, was by definition capable of being more than he was. He awaited some experience, perhaps an experience of something unsettling, to shake him from the monotony of his pleasure.

What Tom awaited, unknowing, was always very close at hand.

We might say this about the city: gray as it was, it always

carried with it the possibility of its other, a city in which greatness, madness and terror shaped the streets and guided the hand of the architect. The other city was always there.

Tom Sorrow had his first suggestion of this other in the person of a young woman with the unusual name of Scilla. He had always imagined himself incapable of a new emotion; he was pleased with the regularity of his passions; but this woman was a promise of depth and distress far beyond what Tom had grown to expect from his daily routine.

Scilla held out, and then retracted, a shadowy promise: I will show you something else.

This was a long time ago. Scilla had disappeared with her promise, and Tom was alone, living, and yet for the first time awake.

As with many men, Tom regarded the workplace as a field for sexual experimentation. He would look on secretaries as creatures brimming over with dim lust, weakness and healthy need. Tom did not always act upon the promise of secretaries, but he liked that they were there, riding the elevators, pressing themselves against the invisible sphere of his private space, pushing the flesh of their legs against his desk as they took notation. Sharpening their nails.

It made the dry, sealed atmosphere of his building bearable, and sometimes even pleasurable. Tom did not like to admit it to himself, but sometimes he felt the same way about the office boys, wondering whether he might not, through the sheer force of his position, be able to tease them away from their adolescent thoughts into some manner of alien activity, perhaps alone with him in the room with the copy machine.

Tom was entranced by the promise of corruption. It was part of the race to the grave.

The story until now has been in pieces. Four long stories, each unwhole, winding in fits and starts across the web that binds us in an effort to contain the truth. For the truth is simply this: the gathering together of all voices. The witnesses brought together, polyphonic in their combined memory, to produce a complete structure. And when each partial story arrives at the end point, a grave that is empty of all but pneumatic angels and bloodied rags, then the story is prepared to walk newly risen in the morning sun.

We have been introduced: I am the brother of your narrator. I am everywhere and nowhere, as a ghost should be, and I am as dead as the chair beneath you. I am older than I was, but I am still a child. A ghost learns. Sees and learns. And though I died a young boy, I understand many things, and I have heard many things. The stories that have moved through me come together in this pale place—this dead and wandering mind—and they make me old, despite my death, despite my youth.

I do not know when it first came to my attention that the young man Tom was distressed. He seemed so cheerful, so prepared, but we should never pretend to know what change will be made in the soul when even the most cheerful young man looks hard into the foundations.

No building suffers gently the revelation of its origins. The Letztesmann Tower was built athwart a grave, and Tom could not remain ignorant of this forever.

It is not good for the dead to be cynical. We have seen all of what there is, the coming and the going, before and aft. Many doors are shut to the living, but the door most firmly closed, so that no light can pass beneath or above or through the mysterious hinge, is the great door that stands between life and the passage beyond. Men speak the word "death," but they do not know whether they speak of a door or a room. Now, in particular, when man looks into reflective things and sees a piteous ape staring back, now is when that door seems final and that room a vaporous dream, a tale told to children.

It is not good for the dead to despair. We have entered that room; we know that death has not simply portals but dominion; we should be happier than man in his fallen animal state, who suspects nothing to await him but life at its least: larvae drawn miraculously from the unpopulated air.

And yet I am not happy here. I am not happy at all.

My only comfort comes from this story, which I have gathered in my walks at night. A story concerning many things, but at the moment this young man, Tom Sorrow, and what he would discover.

Tom had always been of interest to me. I had been drawn to him because he was marked, apart from the others, as a man who did not believe in death. He did not believe that life continued after the grave; he did not believe that it ended; he did not believe in the grave.

These are remarkable, these men: they do not know. Tom was the happiest man I had ever seen.

Scilla would walk carelessly into his office and lean against a wall, silent until Tom had put aside his work to make time for her.

"What do you do with the empty space?" she asked him once.

"Lease it."

"And until it's leased? What do you do with it? Half this tower is empty, and the mall is a tomb."

"Well, I don't know. I guess I think about leasing it; that's what I do. In my line of work, a space is either leased or it's going to be leased; you have to believe; you have to stay optimistic; that's how you make it."

Scilla pursed her black lips, forcing her pity silent. She contemplated Tom, his shining faith, and after a moment she spoke. Scilla spoke carefully, aware that the idea she was presenting to this young man was foreign in the extreme. "Have you considered emptiness? As an end in itself? As something to be celebrated?"

No. No, Tom had not.

Scilla made her cold mouth smile an invitation.

"I think we should spend some time together, Tom. You have to be shown some things."

I watched with interest the education of Tom Sorrow.

You must forgive me if I seem to want to pull fragments together. It is a retrospective impulse: the need to find rhythm in noise, meaning in chance, correspondence in objects and stories perhaps unrelated. And more: it is the overwhelming urge of the melancholic, whose world is rendered always in pieces, rent cloth, absence; the urge to make whole what cannot be made whole, to patch the white spaces between the truth with serviceable lies. I see something in all of this, in these four stories laid out without linear form, an indifferent grid; I see a single point of light, and a moment of damnation.

Pardon me if the grave has made me sentimental. I would

like the path that placed me here to prove capable of charting, a terrain ordered and coherent and charged in its invisible lines with the possibility of a map.

All my life, I wanted my city, my family, the objects around me, to speak as if they had voices; and now, in the silence of the grave, I want to be able to read them. It is perhaps too much to ask.

The city, first. Before we turn to the education of Tom Sorrow—I seem incapable of telling one story merely—let us turn our collective eye to the focus of everything: the towering shadow that defines and renders the city of Toronto, which fixes it to the map like a steel pin through the dried heart of an insect. A tall civic building, all proportion and grid, an obsessive repetitive shadow, both lens and mirror, centrifuge and magnet, the Letztesmann Tower.

Hell is in the details. From a distance, the butterfly is a beautiful creature, a splash of indeterminate color against a drab ground. Beneath the magnifying glass, however, the tiny perfect horror of the thing snaps into focus both before the eyes and behind the mind: the hairs on the carapace, the infernal articulated legs, monstrous head, monstrous thorax, repulsive abdomen, wholly unredeemed by the limp and dusty wings, colorful yes but veined.

The architect Ariel Price made his Letztesmann Tower perfect beneath the most discerning eye, every detail honed and polished to reject the possibility of nature. Before disappearing into his apartment on rue Oberkampf, Price was careful to leave in his wake a final creation, perfectly monstrous in every considered respect, a masterpiece. His tower, the focus of the city, was the complete and irrevocable denial of man.

Price knew that he could never build such a tower in Paris.

The Vulture had tried—was filmed, in fact, expressing his desire to raze Paris and impose a perfect *cimetière*—but he had been thwarted. And when at last an inferior architect had been permitted to place a black tower on the skyline, the gesture had proved insufficient. It was not simply the compromised nature of the tower itself, too timid to express a perfect geometry in opposition to the life of a city: it was the city. Paris was too much alive, had too vast a story, which it told in mythic tones again and again, to permit its reduction by genius. No, the Letztesmann Tower could succeed only in a new city, a city without a sense of itself, a city ripe for colonization. Price would place his vile mirror in the heart of the city of Toronto, and that city would reflect in it and upon it until the tower proved the meaning of the city itself.

True, Price had put a similar tower in the delirious city south of the border, but that city had mocked him. Already dense with height, New York had welcomed Price and dismissed him: his dark tower could do nothing to freeze the heart of that city, already too dense with life to be overwhelmed by a sign of death in its midst. New York conquered death daily, death was carted out in trucks with the garbage, Price could have no dominion.

Canada, however. Newer than the new world. No story, yet, no city to speak of, nothing. Here was a raw place, eager for the knife. Price made for it a monument, a stone, a celebration of the stillborn, a marker to memorialize the unlived. You will look at my building, minions, and despair.

This is how it was intended. There was to be no story. The Letztesmann Tower was to be the antithesis of narrative, a pure grid in three dimensions, utterly new and desolate. But the girl had danced.

I have encountered Theseus Crouch, wandering disconsolate among the dead, his flesh newly burned off, and I know that despite his almost complete failure as a human being, he did make an important discovery, a crucial footnote to the history of built form: that Ariel Price had been derailed in his contemplation, thwarted in his perfection, by the awkward, pathetic dance of a young girl.

The Sabbath is over, and Ariel Price has been given permission to use the fax machine. The hostel has the most sophisticated telecommunications equipment, which the sect employs to maintain contact with colleagues around the world. Ariel Price is impressed, in his madness: could this be the meaning of kabbalah? Access to the innermost network? He has misjudged the Jews.

And he begins to compose a fax.

> Dear Mr. Crouch,
>
> I am pleased to note that you have taken such a profound interest in my life and work. It is clear that you understand the importance of the matters you have chosen to investigate, and even though we may differ in our interpretation of certain events, we are, unbeknownst to you, on the same side. Architecture, the great proving ground of the spirit, is more vast than either of us, my friend, and I admire any man who will step onto that plain to do battle.
>
> I propose that we meet. I shall be in Montreal on business very soon. I would like to sit with you and discuss some of the issues you raise in the first chapter

of your critical biography. You are entitled to come
away, of course, with your own opinions, and I shall
not attempt to pull the wool over your eyes; you are
clearly much too clever to permit that; but I believe
that I retain the capacity to surprise you. Will you meet
with me?

Yours most sincerely,
Ariel Price, architect.

Ariel dials the number in Montreal and watches as the fax machine digests his missive, inch by inch. He taps a swollen knuckle against the plastic device.

The host enters the room from behind him, and gives a little noise. "My friend . . ."

Price spins around, too quickly, then smiles. "Ah. You frightened me."

"There is nothing to be frightened of here."

"No. No, I'm sure there is not."

"Great things. Powerful things, but nothing to be frightened of."

"I am glad. Tell me. You seem to know a great deal about . . . abstract matters. Tell me this: Do you know anything about the laws concerning murder?"

The host raises an eyebrow. "That is not an abstract matter. It is carved in stone. It's clear, my friend: one of the Ten Commandments; maybe you remember."

"Yes, yes, but . . . surely there are circumstances in which it is permitted for a man to kill another man . . ." Ariel's eyes, pink and pleading, smile sheepishly. "War, for instance?"

The host frowns. "Well . . ."

He moves over to the table and pulls out a chair. Ariel snatches the letter from the machine, where it has been regurgitated, and stuffs it hastily in his pocket. The host glances at the bulging pocket.

"Is there any particular reason that you wonder this, my friend, just now?"

"I am just . . . curious."

"Well, there is an obscure section of the laws which deal with, um, pursuit. If a man is being pursued . . . I don't know a lot about this, so you have to take it with a grain of salt . . . but if the man following another man can be designated a 'Pursuer,' then I believe—and this is rare—the followed man has the right to take the other man's life."

Ariel smiles. "What a generous law."

The host looks disturbed. "As I say, I don't know much about this. You should ask the rabbi tonight. Murder is generally, you know, like I say, murder is generally not a good idea. Not a good thing . . ."

"But of course."

"So you will speak to the rabbi, I hope."

"It doesn't really matter. Just curiosity."

"Good."

Theseus Crouch examines the fax with great interest as it crawls spasmodically from his aging machine. A missive from the great man himself. Well. Not entirely unexpected, but nevertheless an event. The stakes have been raised. The game is beginning to get interesting.

Theseus Crouch does not notice that the fax he has received comes not from a small apartment in Paris, but a hostel in

Tzvat. He does not know that the triangle—himself, the competing scholar, the architect—is about to collapse into a duel. All things come together, in the slippery mind of the poet, in the voice of the dead boy who tells stories, and even now the elements are beginning to map onto each other: the competitor and the architect; the aging whore in Tzvat and the young whore in Toronto; the places radically diverse in which Price has erected a tombstone over a labyrinth. All the great cities in the world map onto each other, uneasily, and the story continues.

Ariel Price does not consult the rabbi. Instead, he walks, almost happy, in the light from the falling sun, the sky yellowing with the age of the day like an old manuscript. Ariel Price finds himself singing quietly, under his breath: meaningless syllables. The wind across the mountain carries with it a scent of old paper. A young girl, hair the color of fire, emerges from a stone portal.

Ariel admires the girl. She does not seem local. Her hair is peculiar: one side combed and rich; the other tangled into a storm. A young man is calling her from behind the stone wall; Ariel cannot see him. "Ari," calls the boy—at first Ariel believes the boy is calling him—"Ari, where have you gone?" The girl frowns and, ducking her head, disappears back into the shadows.

You are lost? No, you are not lost. It all comes back to the tower. Through the center of the story, remember, grows a tower, and this will give our journey structure: it grows like a spine right through the center of the mess; it takes the disparate lives, themselves stories, which flower on separate continents, and binds them together as if they were chapters in a book, or floors. The International Style is flexible and versatile, capable of holding in its glass cage every human condition. The base of that tower grows labyrinthine in the architect's mind; the highest reach is a flat and perfect line against the sky; and between these all of life is on display, behind glass. Watch.

THE STORY OF AN EYE

It will never be established whether Ariel Price was born into the New or the Old World. We have details relating to that city of his conception and some clearly pertaining to the city of his birth, but those are abstractions, unhelpful. The birth certificate is American, but we knew that it was obtained some months after the actual birth in a manner hardly sufficient to inspire confidence that we have material proof of the birthplace.

Ariel Price was conceived and born in a city, that much is clear. The Preuss family, Germans transplanted to America (or were they Americans transplanted to Germany?), were an urban family.

This duality haunts us when we encounter every aspect of Price's life, from the work to the politics to the private life, such as it is: he seems at once authentic and derivative, Old and New World, himself and his own flatterer. The person of Price multiplies stereoscopically in our blurred vision, eluding the voice of the narrator, the voice of the biographer, voices speaking through voices. Certainly we know this: Ariel Price was

suspect. The suspicion was that he had spied. Watched.
Seen.

It is not good to be cynical, but I know that education comes only through loss. Education in the deepest sense: knowledge that changes the soul. Tom Sorrow would never learn anything worth knowing while he was still acquiring. And the loss of Scilla was not enough.

Only when the secretaries began to disappear did Tom awaken to the fact that underlies most of human life: the possibility of unhappiness. In his mind he did not yet associate this with the word "death," but Tom would learn.

Michelle was the first to disappear. Tom had hired her the week before, and she had showed great promise: she was efficient, flirtatious, corporate in her dress yet willing, within the bounds of propriety, to take gorgeous risks. Fishnets beneath a prim blue skirt. Scarlet lipstick. A way of dangling a shoe in the midst of dictation, as if it were an exotic bodily ornament designed for temptation, one of those wormlike extrusions found on the foreheads of certain fish. She would do this—dangle her shoe—and he would lose his sentence; it was a game she played.

Tom, then, was satisfied with Michelle, and had hopes of a long, perhaps partially clandestine association. Once, as she was delivering coffee, she leaned close to his ear to examine an object on his desk, and he felt her breath against his shaven skin.

The next day she was gone.

Gone. She did not give notice; she left no indication of her plans; she simply disappeared. Tom was unnerved.

With the disappearance of Michelle, he wondered, as he was

to wonder with the disappearances to follow, whether her leaving was linked in a subtle yet inextricable way to the discovery of that other office dynamic: the silent lust that reinforced and made bearable the relations of power placed upon them by their fixed positions in the hierarchy.

An office building, especially a tall one, is its own cosmos, and it has objective laws: laws of repulsion and attraction, binding the stuff of its being together. Just like any other universe.

Tom wondered.

He was unhappy with the loss of Michelle, but a secretary can always be replaced; this too was a fixed cosmological principle. Still, the substitution of one human for another, especially in matters of lust and corruption, is always an imprecise business, an imperfect fit, leaving small spaces around the edges where the new person does not quite fit the old mold.

Although Alison was needy and flirtatious in her own right, she was not quite Michelle and never would be.

Does it surprise you that I, the dead boy, can tell you of life? You know nothing of death: everything you do, every story you tell is a testament to what you do not know about death, an ignorance bright and more present than your greatest truth; but we the dead know much about life.

We have lived, you see.

And we grow, in death. Is that so surprising? You assume that nothing moves beyond what you can see, but this is simply the bias of the age. Men who lived centuries ago thought differently. And they were right. We grow in death.

Long after your eyes have been eaten, your fingernails will grow long.

I died a youngest son, not yet thirteen, a boy with a lisp and a doomed family. But I have wandered your city for some years since, and in death I have grown and learned new stories. One of which—four of which—I am telling you now.

You should listen to me. The dead have an eye for the essential. Where you see only body, even in architecture, we, the dead, see the eternal.

Tom, as I say, missed Michelle even as Alison strained to fill her every role. He made a concerted effort to discover where she had gone, but there was no trace. Michelle had had few friends, and these few were not close; they assumed she had run off, as she had always dreamed: Michelle had been enthralled by the posters in tour offices, the deep and alien blue. Perhaps she had saved some money and simply gone.

Tom, even as he kissed Alison's neck, did not believe it.

"You're not with me, Tom."

"Mm?"

"You're all far away. What's up?"

"S'nothing . . ." he mumbled against her pink ear, and she giggled.

"That felt funny. Tom, what are you thinking about?" Tom gently extricated himself from his secretary's warm arms, and sat contemplatively on the edge of the desk.

"I don't know, Alison. I don't know really. I've never thought of myself as the sort of guy who develops attachments. To people. Especially people I work with, who work for me: it's always seemed a foolish thing to do. Care about them . . ."

Alison took this the wrong way and was pleased. She kissed

him. "That's sweet. It's okay, you know; I don't think it's going to affect our work relationship . . ."

Tom shook his head, a bit too vigorously. "No. I . . . no, I wasn't talking about this. This is fine. I was talking about something else."

Alison pulled away. "Oh."

"It's bothering me that Michelle just disappeared. You didn't know her. She was the secretary before you. Disappeared."

The next morning Alison was gone. Tom never saw her again.

> *Tiny Ariel Price was effeminate and sickly, ominous attributes in a family desperate to produce an heir. His bones were outlandish. He was delicate, almost bird-like, as if designed less for survival as the son and grandson of stonemasons than for unaided flight. His mother was slightly in awe of her preternatural boy, an awe tempered subliminally by revulsion; when she picked young Ariel up from the crib he weighed less than nothing.*
>
> *Ariel's father, Festus Preuss, records in his diary that his wife has made a "startling confession": "I feel as if I have given birth to something almost immaterial. A malevolent sprite."*
>
> *Might we find in Ariel's rarefied flesh the ineluctable urge toward weighty creation? In his youthful stature (later he would grow monstrously tall, but he remained until sixteen the shortest boy in his class) the obsession with tallness? And in his mother's distance, the later pathological need for female affirmation?*

The family name "Preuss" was in flux for much of this period but appears on Ariel's birth certificate in the Germanic spelling later rejected by the whole family: Ariel was not always "Ariel Price."

On the day that he left his father's shop, never to return, young Ariel filed to have his name changed to the American "Price."

Festus Preuss was a wealthy stonemason, not as unusual as might be thought: fine craftsmen were in great demand early in Festus's career, and he became a purveyor of gargoyles to the growing bourgeoisie. The nation was obsessed with the Gothic, after centuries of dismissing the style as barbaric, and Festus Preuss proved uniquely capable of translating that obsession into credible mantelpieces.

Many have credited the austerity of Ariel's aesthetic with an almost Freudian animadversion to his father's taste, but I hope in the course of this biography to lay that misconception permanently to rest: the modern, as conceived by the son Ariel, is fully Gothic in its impulse: morbid, thanatocentric, nocturnal. Ariel Price simply saw no special need for gargoyles and tracery in the accomplishment of this grotesque project.

And it is no accident, when we examine the later life of Ariel Price, that the obsession with the Gothic that was to create the family fortune and lift his father from proletarian origins was an obsession predicated upon a fiction. A novel, to be precise. The Continent had been seduced by a brutal story, a winding tale of architecture, rape and miscegenation, an unholy account of the clandestine marriage between the sacred and the profane in the creation of the medieval sensibility.

One secretary in particular haunted Tom Sorrow: Lara, thoughtful Lara, who had read Artaud at her desk.

One afternoon, at five-thirty, Tom was running to catch the elevator. The doors were closing. He saw Lara standing alone in the car. "Hold the door, Lara . . ."

The look on her face. She did not move. An expression of transcendental terror, fear in response to something more frightening than Tom could ever imagine. "Lara?"

And as the doors closed—he could not catch them, and she did not move to stop them—Lara cried out once, with a voice that Tom could never recall without closing his eyes in pity: "Sanctuary!"

The doors closed on the girl and Tom never saw her again. But as he watched the numbers descend in the tiny window above the closed elevator doors, Tom was seized with a suspicion that he could not seem to shake, one that merely grew every time he turned the incident over in his mind: the secretary and office boys were being sacrificed to something, something that lived in the maze beneath the Letztesmann Tower.

It was this thought, revolving and deepening in the increasingly unhappy consciousness of Tom Sorrow, that grew into a full and profound education, changed him and marked him and gave him entrance to life.

Tom took to long meditative walks at night. He began to cultivate a new nocturnal persona, thoughtful and melancholic, aware in a way he would not permit himself to be at his desk. The buildings themselves became something else at night: no longer efficient, no longer even useful, they thinned to an abstraction and became pure form.

Tom, as he walked between them, began to intuit the other reason for architecture. Tom Sorrow had never heard of Ariel Price. He knew that someone must have designed the building in which he worked, that somebody's thought had shaped the path of his daily routine, but he had never stopped to consider the precise nature of that tyrant.

At night, however, it was different. Tom discerned in the perfection of the black shadow against the night sky the gesture of a complex and perhaps not entirely pleasant artist.

Tom, whose days were blindly caught in the tidal movements of economy, was only at night fully aware of the possibility, the reality of loss.

If my voice seems to come to you from a great distance, it is only because it does. The distance between you, living reader, and me cannot be measured with ordinary tools—calipers, rulers, string—but must be intuited *per impossibile* like the vastness that separates a desperate from a happy man.

And Tom Sorrow, you must remember, was the latter when I met him. I met him on an evening when this happiness was most precarious, the young salesman in his shimmering bubble of joy contemplating the lancet offered by a cruel woman, her counterfeit of love. I saw him move through this encounter made wiser but not yet unhappy. That was long ago. The woman then withdrew into the periphery of his bright life. He thought of her, too often perhaps, but was still remarkable in his joy.

Perhaps it requires an observer from my distance to put the

pieces together, to draw the careful line that links apparently disparate poles in the diagram: the hard demise of Tom's unnatural joy, and the protracted mysterious sojourn, much earlier, with that morbid woman.

Scilla had never emerged without first painting her lips some poisonous color, as if she had recently kissed something dead. She applied fresh poison to her lips before visiting Tom in his office, which she did with increasing frequency now that she understood the possibilities breathing dormant in the Letztesmann Tower.

Scilla never mentioned to Tom the boy with the bleeding forehead, what she had seen that night in the underground mall. Scilla did not yet want Tom to know what lay beneath the space he was leasing.

And so, the beginnings of Tom's education—the process would not deepen until long after Scilla's departure—took place far from the Letztesmann Tower. Scilla wanted to teach him to see before she gave him something to look at.

She took him west, along College Street and Queen Street, into back rooms and onto rooftops, where his red suspenders stood out like poisonous coloration. "Don't worry, sweetheart. No one's going to eat you. Nobody would want to, in those clothes . . ."

Tom was always cheerful, of course, but nervous. Scilla introduced him to people his own age who were much less happy with their lot than he was. These were young men and women who had no hope unless their desperate plunge from society were redeemed by genius or faith, and most of them possessed neither. They stared at Tom with special loathing: he was even less than they were, for he had declined even to take the plunge. And some of them, secretly of course, wanted what he had. What they too had once had, before they rejected it as banal.

Scilla's acquaintances seemed always on the retreat from gentrification. Everywhere they tentatively made home and decorated to indicate their rejection of wealth was inevitably coopted by the wealthy. Scilla was unique in that she had chosen to reenter the rejected domain, to occupy and subvert it. And Tom was her way in.

She introduced Tom to various toxins, each refined to elicit a different mode of confusion. The green plant, the black sap, the white page printed with Gnostic symbols, serial emblems of madness. Tom was game. And he proved remarkably impervious to confusion. "Wow," he would say. "This is really something. "

But Scilla knew that she was planting seeds. Someday what she had placed in Tom's soul would take him like the vine, slow and relentless, the vine that splits stone.

And when the secretaries began to disappear, Tom's education began to reveal its method.

Always, Scilla would inquire about the emptiness. For despite Tom's constant efforts to people the tomb, the Letztesmann Tower remained largely empty.

I could see, from my intimate yet distant vantage point, that Scilla, even as she taught Tom, was losing her stomach for the lesson. Tom was changing, but Scilla too was changing, as a consequence of her midnight encounter.

As she tried with all her wiles and bitter strength to pull Tom down, Scilla found that she occupied a less and less depressed terrain.

No, the only character in this drama to seek truth in the

very lowest places, despite Scilla's efforts to discern his impenetrable heart, was Ariel Price. And the revelation of the Dead Sea before Price's ascent into the mountains of Galilee would guide him in those final terrible moves in the game. That desperate end game, two spiders, one web, Ariel Price and Theseus Crouch on level ground at last: facing each other on the plateau.

Ariel Price booked a ticket, by fax, for the city of Montreal.

Scilla educated Tom Sorrow.

Jernigan Noer moved, ancient almost, through the coffee and used clothing of Queen Street, seeking a woman with poisonous lips.

Turning, the crystal has again caught the light, and bent it to a shape hard with the rule of optics.

THE TYRANNY OF GLASS

As a biographer, it is perhaps ironic that I am forced to question the motive for reconstructing the urban landscape as a conversation between voyeurs and victims, the Privileged Eye and the Hapless Object. Still, I have no choice but to investigate this aspect of the Price for-

mula: where we can argue that tallness was a condition imposed upon him by the vulgarity of his clients, we cannot deny that transparency was his own: glass is a material extruded from the very soul of Ariel Price.

The predicament of the watcher. None of the self-styled "biographies" mentions the name of a young girl known to have danced, unwittingly, for Ariel Price, in the public space spread like a specimen beneath a microscope before the lens of Price's office window in the Letztesmann Tower.

You may search the indexes of all the major historians fruitlessly, not least because we do not know whether the young girl had a last name. She is unremembered. Had I never met the boy, Joshua Darlow, who had made the Letztesmann Tower his haunt and personal obsession, I might never have been privileged to hear the name "Bethany." And had I never investigated the circumstance of this girl, unremembered, an entire chapter in the history of modernism might have remained forever unwritten.

Every life can be read through the prism of a single incident. This is not so much a biographical as an optical device, and it is perhaps a construct—so much fiction—but like all fiction it is an instrument of revelation.

I have spent many years wondering when my research would yield up the incident through which the Price life might be refracted to best advantage, and I had almost despaired of finding it when I met a young man with an injured brow standing quietly in the lobby of the Letztesmann Tower. Through him I met a small network of friends, none noteworthy as historical fig-

ures except for their shared concern with a single for-
gotten incident, an act on the periphery of history; the
encounter between a great man and a young girl in an
empty space.

Scilla's world was frigid but oddly accommodating. It was an unwritten assumption underlying their casual society: that the group was amorphous and shadowy, permitting always quiet additions at the margin. Most of her acquaintances described themselves in terms of precisely these categories—shadow and margin—and it was a matter of honor among them to respect, always, the fact of exile from society. When a citizen fell through the cracks, whether through choice or fate, they were not there precisely to welcome him, but they were there.

Jernigan Noer was permitted to move among them. Questions were not asked. Jernigan was dissipated, clearly, pained but stoical. His clothes were musty and had stories of their own, stories he had never been told. In short: he was one of them. Perhaps older than most, although there were men and women among them whose poverty was no longer youthful poverty and whose anger had hardened in that way which permits no alchemical reversion, to bitterness. He was quiet and unattractive, and he posed no sexual threat. Insofar as anyone was welcome among them, Jernigan Noer was welcome.

Scilla was intrigued. Jernigan sought her out, and when he had found her, he focused in upon her with an intensity she had not witnessed since those important days with Campbell. What he seemed to want, first and foremost, was conversation. And quietly, he had much to say.

When he spoke, however, his face did not move with the vigor Scilla had come to expect from such intensity of verbal expression. The flesh of his face seemed frozen, unreal at the surface, so that the words alone were left to convey his meaning. Even his body seemed too cold for gesture. One arm in particular almost never moved; he kept his left arm at his side like a dumb implement, a limb whose use he had outgrown and forgotten in the course of evolution.

Jernigan had a coarse and ugly beard; Scilla found herself wondering what that mask of hair concealed. Did the lips perhaps move too tellingly? Was the chin weak and expressive? Was Jernigan afraid that his face if shaved would belie his robotic manner?

Or was it something else?

They lit fires in abandoned lots, squatted close to the ground and spoke, their eyes meeting sometimes in complicit recognition, like the merging of shadows.

Scilla was changing. And the direction of that change was increasingly dictated by this graceless being, awkward and more articulate than anyone she had met in years.

Jernigan Noer was capable of putting words together to form dreams: not simply ideas, but ideas with profound intent, willed ideas whose orientation pointed convincingly toward grand things, even greatness, completion. Although he was clearly suffering and probably lost, Scilla sensed in his presence flickering moments of that one attribute so painfully absent in the hungry pose of so many of her acquaintances: genius. Scilla still believed in genius. She knew that the concept was old-fashioned, and thought by many politically suspect—redolent as it was of mastery and authorial will—but she found it a necessary category, for without the possibility of genius there was nothing to make sense of her fallen world. Nothing. And Scilla was hardly one to disdain mastery.

Jernigan Noer, slouched in his tweed coat, alone suggested to Scilla that what they each pretended might actually be achieved. He even gave hints that he had once achieved it himself. That once, in the dim receding past, before his body and face had frozen into grotesque immobility, Jernigan Noer had made something.

"Scilla," he said as the fire put unreal warmth into his colorless skin, "I think you agree with me. This pavement is a window. This filth is pollen. If you follow this shitty street past that final piece of concrete rotting at the corner, the streetlights open into flesh."

Not having any precise sense of what he was saying, Scilla did nevertheless agree.

"Jernigan, what are you going to do?"

"I don't know. I don't know yet."

"Will you let me help you?"

Jernigan sat quietly on his haunches. He rocked almost imperceptibly—Jernigan Noer never made large movements—and sucked in air over his tongue, testing it.

"When I'm ready to make something, you're going to be my first lieutenant. You're going to manage the stage. You're going to find the space and watch it for us, and when we have put it together, you're going to help me move it in. You're going to be very good."

Scilla had a space in mind.

Izzy and Arianna walk the nameless neighborhood in silence, space between them. This is the preternatural calm, the sanity that descends in the wake of bitter words.

Unexpectedly, she takes Izzy's hand. They walk like this for some time, his hand held lightly in hers. When she speaks at last, her voice is level and weary.

"You don't have to put up with me."

"Don't say that."

"I know that I'm not stable. I know that I make people unhappy. You don't have to put up with me."

Izzy holds her hand tightly. "It's not a question of putting up with you. I want you to feel comfortable . . . I want you to feel safe with me."

She pulls her hand away. "I never will."

The orange light from the streetlamp isolates them against the pavement, spotlit unreal.

"You don't know that."

Tiny pieces of glass glitter improbably in the pavement, catch and reflect the orange light. Some time ago the city builders began to roll glass into the stuff of roads, trying to make the street a window.

"Will you come back with me, Ari?"

"I'm not going to sleep with you."

"That's not what I'm asking."

"I'll sleep beside you, but I'm not going to sleep with you."

Izzy and Arianna walk, closer now, sometimes touching, and the pavement sparkles beneath their quiet feet.

Ariel had the dream again. Two buildings, bracketing existence: one on either side, a lover on each arm. He had made the city tall and was prepared to walk away.

Wearing a long coat, with the collar turned up—the same coat in which he had been photographed, famously, conversing with the Vulture in front of Deux Magots—Ariel took one last look at the high and lonely window, bright and lonely and his, and turned from his dark creation to stride with great steps down the wide road that led away from his city.

The dream would end, often, with this: Ariel striding, aware of the figure that he cut in his lengthy, heroic garment, the cloth whirling about his legs as he moved proudly through the night on long legs, the city that he had made diminishing behind him, finished.

But then, on this rather different night, during which his crippled assistant was, even then, violating the flesh of the young woman Ariel had chosen to honor with his lust, the dream found a new and disturbing conclusion.

As Ariel strode through the darkness, he heard the sound of steel against pavement: the scraping that sends sparks arcing into the night. A vile whore stepped out from the shadows of a Dumpster and blocked his path. She was crawling with insects, and her light garment was smeared with road filth. Ariel raised a fist to smite her, but she simply stood, at her full height, and allowed the hood to fall from her tall head, revealing the face obscured. It was the visage of a heavenly messenger. In his mind, Ariel quickly cycled through the order of angels, discovering as he reviewed the hierarchy that this—his angel—was at the very top of the list. As he might have expected. The angel that confronted Ariel Price, to deliver a message, was the very best type of angel. The most important by far.

Behind her, also emerging from shadow, were three women, roped by the neck to a small boat, which they dragged across the pavement, its keel screeching in misery.

"I am Mary," said the angel. "And this," she said, indicating one of the three women, "is Mary. And this too is Mary. And this," indicating the last, a small black woman with the calm face of wisdom but disquieting eyes, "is Sarah. We are the three Saints Mary, and this, our servant, is Saint Sarah."

Ariel Price regarded the serving woman with distaste: a servant, and a Negro, a saint? But the woman looked back at him with eyes that made his soul shrink in its container like a withered penis.

"I shall keep you safe in your travels, for you have built a most auspicious and extreme city," said the first Mary, in the guise of a whore. "I am your angel, Ariel Price. I am for you. But—"

Yes? thought Ariel. But what? Ought there to be restrictions upon his angelic companionship? His city was very good.

"But I must insist that you go now, along this great way, and do not turn back. Do not once turn to look at the city that you have made, for it is finished."

Ariel's lip curled in disdain. He was not accustomed to restrictions: certainly, nothing heavenly had stood in his way before. "Thank you," he said curtly. "I shall consider your advice."

"I am not advising you, Ariel Price: I am insisting. Go now."

Ariel stared coldly at the angel, who was garbed, it must be confessed, as a whore, and turned with deliberate insolence to stare fully upon the city that he had made.

The angel cried once, with great anguish, and the foul rags fell from her, revealing her in naked glory so bright that Ariel would have been ashamed to look upon her, except that he was not. Ariel was gazing at his city.

And so that the architect did not turn capriciously and look upon the nakedness of the angel, the angel miraculously grew hair to cover her angelic body in its entirety—a thick coat of hair from her neck to her ankles—and then, like a sleek and perfect animal, the angel rose on a warm current of air, and disappeared into the black sky. The other women, Mary and Mary and Sarah, clung to the side of their small boat. It too rose on a swirling invisible tide and floated off into the night like a lost balloon.

Ariel had seen nothing of this. He was sick with watching something else: the two tallest towers, his pride and accomplishment, had, at the moment of his turning, changed to pillars of white crystal. And then, as he briefly admired the effect that these glittering pillars created against the night sky, a torrent of rain swept through the firmament, drenching the architect and his new city, and the white towers began to lose their form. The edges went soft, like the edges of ancient mountains, and then the tops washed away, and then the towers in their entirety melted, slowly but inexorably, and drained to the gutter, reduced to watery salt. And then they were gone.

Ariel, shivering in cold and horror, stood alone.

PART FOUR: PANOPTICON

It is always Judas who writes the biography.

—OSCAR WILDE

The stage is bare except for a long grave carved into the earth of the floor. The contents of this grave are reflected to the audience in a giant mirror suspended above the floor at an angle of forty-five degrees. Empty grave clothes lie abandoned in the center of the pit. At the head and foot of the grave sit ANGELS: the first fixes a bicycle; the second peels an orange.

SAINTES-MARIES kneels at the lip of the grave. She stares directly into the suspended mirror, i.e., into the eyes of the audience. Deliberately, with slow ritualistic movements, she smears her makeup. Her lipstick widens into a smiling gash. Her mascara bleeds into black tears, arrows pointing toward the origin: the vulnerable, soon-to-be-martyred eyes.

VOICE:
Don't touch me. Don't touch me. Don't touch me.

SAINTES-MARIES turns to the source of the VOICE.

VOICE:
Mary.

SAINTES-MARIES (*in a monotone*):
Teacher.

The VOICE continues to utter this single word, "Mary," but the quality of the VOICE erodes, as if conveyed by a radio with the reception going off. One of the ANGELS picks up a small radio receiver and fiddles with the dial, but the VOICE disappears into static. The ANGEL shrugs.

SAINTES-MARIES puts her hands to her eyes. She opens her mouth in a silent scream. When she takes her hands away and places them out, palms up, in an attitude of supplication, there is a bleeding eye on either palm. Her eyelids, neither open nor closed, hang like stage curtains over an empty space.

The first ANGEL retires his bicycle pump. The second savors a slice of orange.

We the dead are the confluence of narrative. Every story is a race to the grave. And when they arrive, the stories, separately or together, we are there to collect them. I can tell every story that was ever told—there is only one—and I have many voices. Yes, I know the story in that novel, the one that made the Continent reappraise the hulking cathedrals at the center of their lives, but as I tell it I cannot always separate it out from other stories, each delirious with pain, ornate with dancing girls and voyeurs, every city approximately and incestuously mapping onto every other. There is only one city, and there is only one story.

In the cold apartment—the wall now whole, but the midnight air still finding its way in, through cracks and imperfect windows—Izzy and Arianna lie in bed. He is almost naked, wrapped in the comforter, but she is fully clothed. They say nothing. For hours, however, they are both awake, and the bed is charged with suspicion. Izzy squeezes his eyes tight, trying to will away the haunting proximity of this woman, warm, beside him. On his forehead light moisture. Arianna's eyes are open, and she is calm; she studies the ceiling, the places where Izzy has had to paint over discolored patches where the rain found its way through the plaster. He does not know much about shelter, does he.

Stein Foregutt spent little time summing up the situation. Pasty officials, nervous and confused in the commission of a task not prescribed by their bureaucratic experience, clutched papers, fiddled with pens, and looked up occasionally, with glances considerably less perspicuous, less carnivorous than his own. Stein understood them, but they did not understand him.

"It is a prestigious commission," said one, "you should be, um, pleased, I would think . . ."

"I'll decide what does and does not flatter me."

This remark sent them into a flurry of clutching and fiddling: were they going to be treated to one of Stein Foregutt's legendary dramas? His persona—much better known than his architecture—was fearsome. Foregutt's peculiar talent was to convert uncouth displays of temper into aesthetic myth. He had been born with a rare aptitude for rudeness, one of those souls incapable of shame, but this talent—which might well have fated him to a reputation for vulgarity—was combined with a unique ability to interpret acts and things in a way that seemed to take, permanently, in the public consciousness. As the self-proclaimed oracle, Foregutt was in a position to explain what difficult circumstances meant, and specifically what his own tempestuous displays portended in the grand line of historical gestures, a respectable lineage traced from Diogenes through Rimbaud.

"I'll decide. Thank you." Foregutt smiled. His smile was disarmingly genuine and served to erase even the most recent fears: Foregutt was good and bad cop, combined in one monstrous charming figure. "But you are right. A prison for the great Ariel Price. As an architect, of course I am aware of the . . . significant precursors."

The bureaucrats smiled, hesitant.

"Only one great prison has been dedicated, in this century, to the punishment of a single architect, and—yes, certainly, you are correct—it is an honor to be the designer chosen to incarcerate the great Ariel Price."

A long, hopeful silence.

"Of course, the budget you have presented is ludicrous. Barely sufficient to cover my personal fee."

One of the bureaucrats bit his lip so hard that a single drop of blood stained his beard.

It was not an ordinary interview. Stein Foregutt was accustomed to young, eager students, desperate for work and prestige by association. This man was old. How old it was impossible to say: he was physically enigmatic. Foregutt, with his eye for cladding and purity of materials, sensed immediately an adjustment of the essence, perhaps a long and successful regime of plastic surgery. The man had military posture, but it seemed false, as if a steel rod had been inserted in the spine. And the skin across his face—what he could see of it beneath the beard—was too tight, altogether too stretched and transparent; something had been made here.

"I'm sorry. Your name again?"

The man hesitated for a moment. "Jernigan. Jernigan Noer."

"Jernigan. And . . . may I ask you, Jernigan, why it is you wish to work with me?"

Another long silence.

"I'm interested in the project."

"The project. And which particular project has captured the imagination of Jernigan Noer?"

In a whisper: "The Price Prison."

Foregutt nodded with new respect. He, Foregutt, could appreciate fully the significance of this project, but he hardly expected anyone else to comprehend the irony of the commission.

"You understand that I don't pay my assistants."

"I understand."

"And that you will be expected to work at least as hard—harder—than you would for money."

Jernigan Noer smiled, an expression alien to the physics of his facial skin.

"Your reputation precedes you, Mr. Foregutt."

Foregutt glowered, then closed his eyes and smiled. "Yes. I suppose it does." He glanced down at the résumé in front of him. "You did very well in school. Very well. Impressive. Some . . . years ago, however. I don't know of your practice."

"You wouldn't. I took myself out of the field, deliberately, soon after graduation. I wasn't ready." Noer paused, and stared unblinking at the bad boy architect. Foregutt was unnerved by the intensity of his gaze. "I'm ready now."

Foregutt and Noer. The famous enfant terrible was handsome, in a calculated way: black hair casually permitted to grow wild about the shoulders, two days worth of specially trimmed beard on the grand jaw, tiny circular spectacles to add the necessary note of idiosyncrasy, to preclude anyone mistaking the gorgeous Foregutt for a male model. And the interviewee: the beard seemed to conceal a constructed face, unreal.

When I met the architect Jernigan Noer, he was part of neither your world nor mine. Remorse had made him transparent, a creature through which the daylight passed, a fabric worn thin. Every movement he made seemed to cause him pain, and yet I could not discern whether this pain was physical—certainly, he had undergone many operations and the scars were prominent—or whether the simple fact of animation was enough to remind him of what he had done, albeit unwittingly, when he was somebody else.

He had the kind of dignity that I associate with genius, even though it was clear that he was a thwarted genius, that he had made nothing of his life.

Jernigan had immersed himself in the study of prisons. They were a revelation. In the articulation of the cage for its fellow citizen, the human has lavished all the passion and ingenuity of its species, and the unfolding of that story—the story of unfreedom and its engineering—is the narrative that encompasses in its microcosmic trajectory all stories. The bars at the gates of Eden made all the world a prison and every human body its own mobile cage. This was the first lesson learned and internalized by Jernigan Noer: the simple yet ingenious propensity to place cages within cages, to overbuild unfreedom so that it was circumscribed within a wider realm of unfreedom, so that even the escaping prisoner would find himself, after a moment flushed with the false recognition of liberty, still caged.

In the incarceration of the human, Jernigan discovered a punishment more horrible than execution: imprisonment is life taken while lived; it is death with the admixture of duration, death with dimension.

Jernigan drew feverishly: cages within cages, and each cage containing within it, like a hologram, the tyranny of the whole. He had once been made to design, unknowingly, the place of execution, and he put special zeal into the willful design of this: the place of punishment.

He quickly drew Scilla into his plans.

A place of punishment must be, first and foremost, a theater. Justice must be seen to be done. A man punished for watching must be punished by watching.

The eyes of Saintes-Maries. For witnessing, the punishment was blindness.

In this way, one whore is discerned from another. The whore unredeemed, Ariel Price, who had made the city tall because he was, in his own words, whore to the whims of his client; and the whore redeemed. One to be watched, his sight turned inward upon himself and augmented by thousands of eyes; the other to have her eyes torn out, left sightless except for the light carried within: the light of association and memory.

Redemption is optical.

Ariel Price charges through the streets of Montreal in a taxi that skids wildly in the packed snow. The driver wishes to slow down, but Ariel will not permit it; the driver bends beneath the fierceness of the architect's resolve. Ariel will meet this biographer.

The great man has never been to Montreal. Yes, he designed

a suite of buildings here, but this did not require a visit: they were black towers, indistinguishable from the towers he had placed at the heart of every other city. Ariel Price had been informed of the cultural knots woven through life in Montreal, the unique concerns of its citizenry, but he had noted rightly that architecture is above this notion of culture with a small "c." Let them have towers.

Most of the housing to either side is awkward and idiosyncratic: two- and three-story structures with exterior ironwork, peculiar stairs of iron designed to convey occupants to their front doors on the second and third floors of stubby buildings. How perverse that even now, late in the twentieth century, supposedly civilized buildings do not know to tame and internalize the vagaries of circulation.

Although Price has lived some years in Paris, he cannot untangle the accent he encounters at the airport in Montreal: they might as well be speaking another language. Coming from Israel, Price is reminded how little the inessential aspects of human life matter to him, how little it concerns him whether the world is old or new; whether the dialect is Hebrew, Arabic or French; whether the locals have developed over centuries their own quaint notions of domestic style.

The biographer lives on "The Plateau." Ariel expects to find, in the center of the city, a dramatic mesa, but is disappointed. Similarly, the famed "Mountain" at the center proves little more than a landscaped hill. For all his famous glorification of the minimal, Ariel Price has never been fond of understatement.

Ariel Price approaches rue Esplanade, where Theseus Crouch maintains a small apartment.

The team assembled to discuss the room in which the great architect would be incarcerated. Silence reigned. Ariel would later guess rightly, that his cell was designed by another architect. And this architect, the fabulous Stein Foregutt, now weighed in his mind the gravity of the commission, and was somber. This mattered. The team waited nervously for him to speak. At his left sat Jernigan Noer, project architect for the prison. But Foregutt did not yet have anything to say. Nothing to say.

The architect stared at the blank notepaper in front of him. He rolled his pencil back and forth along the desk. He ran his finger along the edge of the paper. So quickly that he did not have time to wince in pain, the paper slid into his skin, searing, and blood pressed out in a thick drop on the fingertip, staining the paper a deep orange-red. He froze, tensing, and stared at this. The students also stared, appalled. The architect drew two lines on the paper; they met at the bottom in a sharp point; he put his finger to his mouth, drew blood, held up the paper and said: "This is the section."

Bethany climbs her way through tears to the open grave, where they have placed the pierced body of the protagonist. Sarah is already there, hands folded, silenced in the middle of her story. To the side stands a woman with a halo, weeping blood. The halo is not a shining ring, as Bethany has always imagined, but a circular window, turning, through which eternity blazes grimly. A thorn window. The woman stands human beneath her halo, destined by her story to remain fixed here in the tableau forever: flesh riven by significance, pinned bleeding to the canvas by arms too strong to hold anything merely human.

God have pity on the girl caught even briefly in His gaze.

The pieces of the story, as I have found them scattered jigsaw in the street, are these.

1. The ride into Jerusalem. Saintes-Maries, least and greatest of the followers, feels a cross sear like a brand into the space between her shoulders. The next morning she will awaken scarred. She will develop a unique sympathy for animals, her eyes meeting the eyes of the donkey with a spark of dumb intelligence.
2. The dinner. Lamb.
3. The kiss.
4. The mall.
5. The tower.

A PARALLEL LIFE

These are the pieces. Slivers in the flesh. Days that get beneath the surface of the body, sing there, grow thick with infection like pearls. Hard memories. Sand.

He has come up from the Sinai Desert. No sand there, but stone the color of thirst. He has stared out across the Gulf of Aqaba into the lights of Jordan, pinpricks of light, tiny, alien, as small and abstract as the stars. Standing with soldiers in the bus through the Negev, he was pushed up against forearms so strong and dark and male that he felt sick with himself. Weak. His body has become weak. His soul has bled into his flesh, and now there is only one kind of pain. He carried his shaken self up through the cold Negev into the green irrigation of Galilee, wept at the sight of leaves, was scorned by soldiers and found himself here on a sacred mountain, lost in the holy city of Tzvat.

Here he may heal. And if he cannot heal, he prays that he may change, become different from himself, other from this creature who is merely sick with pain. He has given all of himself away, except for this, and he is nothing more. Arianna. Look what you have done to the rest of him.

The morning air slows the hands, even here in the library, but he can write. He has come through the lowest place on earth, shore of the Dead Sea warm like the core, but this is the top of a mountain. It is February. They have had snow in Tel Aviv for the first time in years. He is being punished.

It is easy to lose himself in the ritual. What he has not lost already. He is going through the motions of Orthodoxy, foreign and also familiar, and what was senseless is now beginning to make sense. Posters on the wall give him pieces of theory. The reasons why. He washes his hands with a special two-handled jug, keeps Kosher, sings songs whose meaning escapes him, but whose melody has meaning. The reasons why. Once there was a Temple to mediate between us, Jahweh and his childish tribe, but the Temple was destroyed. Now every man must make his body into a temple, perform the many personal rituals in place of the sacrifice. Alone with a God whose face is turned away. The logic is unlike anything he was taught to know, but here it makes clear, transcendent sense. He has been superstitious for two years now. Since the day he met Arianna. His superstitions are growing hard within him, taking the shape of narrative, and the firmness, the stony structural consistency, of faith.

It is easy to lose himself in ritual, but here in the library, alone with his silence, the pen cold in his hand, he finds that his self comes flooding back. Faith simply gives meaning to the pain. No comfort, but meaning.

There is plenty of time, here at the hostel, to write. He is expected to study, once or twice a day, but the classes are not rigorous, and the rest of the time is his own. He is writing a story about the woman who cut him adrift from himself and his adopted city, who sent him wounded across the landscape to search for another city, who sent him here.

He has taken to writing the story of Bethany in the third person. As if she had loved and broken another man, not him. He does this to create distance. He watches her with this other man, whose name is Cosimo Neri, and he feel that he is in some crucial way external to the dance: not the choreographer, but the audience. He is outside of the suffering that passes between them. He is jealous.

Ariel Price, when he was led out of the courtroom, was heard to sigh to his lawyer, "I knew from the beginning that I would have to be crucified."

Stein Foregutt, when the magazines indicated the degree to which he had accepted favors in return for his considered decision not to write the unofficial Price biography, complained to a prominent critic, "This is nothing short of a crucifixion."

Saintes-Maries was not permitted to be with him when they shattered the bones in his hands and feet. She knew that he had been flayed and humiliated, and this was a torment to know, but still she wanted so much to be with him at the end, even if his suffering were too much for the watching heart to bear: it seemed only just—a part of the greater symmetry—that she should die for his pain.

The materialists have a great deal to say about crucifixion. We know the force required to drive steel through flesh, and the added impact necessary to force even a sharp nail through young bone; all of this can be calculated; the calculations are not particularly complex, the theory culled mostly from Newtonian physics and early anatomical studies; this is not difficult.

We have a much more complex understanding of pain, however.

Only after the ambitious experiments undertaken in Europe do we know the precise limits to suffering and endurance: how much the human body can withstand before it ceases, in any meaningful way, to be human; what changes take place in that part of the body that governs consciousness as pain is increased systematically beyond specified thresholds. The Gate Theory of Pain suggests that the moment of excruciation—the moment, for instance, when the bones in the hand are bent by the nail precisely to the limit of flexibility and shatter—is accompanied by the opening of a so-called gate in the pineal gland. This simple biological function, the swinging of a gate upon a hinge, is thought to flood the central nervous system with searing light, described by some as roughly similar to the circumstance of the retina at the moment of sun blindness, when light from the sun has had the opportunity to focus, concentrated, on a single spot until it has burned a small hole in the optic nerve.

The materialists generally shy away from the more extravagant descriptions of this process, in which this flood of light is compared, for instance, to a great turning rose window, the bleeding eye of a cathedral pouring fire into the congregation. This is not thought to correspond, rigorously, to the scientific method. Still, we know that the angle of the spine, as the feet are turned and hammered into place, is sufficient—when combined with the weight of the body, even taking blood loss into account, as the cross is raised and jerked into its foundation hole—to throw the discs out of alignment, pressing with the force of a dog's jaw against the crying spinal tissue, so that the swinging Gate comes to rest at a position of maximal aperture, affording an intolerable exposure to the light of being. Here again the most strict positivists remove themselves from speculation, but less rigorous materialists are willing to venture that this exposure is irreversible and incommensurable with the equilibrium required to keep the human brain functioning within the parameters loosely designated as "sanity."

Not much is known about the effects of humiliation. That crucifixion does not simply represent a limit to the possibility of human suffering in a strictly biological sense, but also combines this special torment with a superaddition of social devastation, in which the powerful spiritual leader—once designated "teacher" and even "king"—is made to suffer a punishment associated with thieves: the full effect of this augmented social dimension to the suffering has yet to be measured, and there are those who insist that it cannot properly be reproduced in the laboratory with satisfactory rigor.

Also to be taken into account is the perverse possibility that the "teacher" in question might, through a peculiar idiosyncrasy, find the company of thieves either a neutral or even an ameliatory factor: this too complicates the equation.

Saintes-Maries' gifts were not mathematical. She could measure certain human quantities, but her skill was intuitive. In this sense, it did not matter so much that she was not present to gather empirical evidence of her teacher's suffering. Nor when they put out her eyes did it particularly alter her ability to see what mattered.

NO LIFE BEARS SCRUTINY.

These words are engraved over the cell door. Ariel Price stops to read them, but the guard shoves him brutally, and he stumbles forward into the darkness. A face like an ax. The guard, thinks Ariel Price, has a face like an ax. And then the sliding noise of a great bolt, steel on oil, click, and the unlight is perfect.

The great architect lies, breathing, where he has fallen. He feels about the space with trembling fingers and ponders this: the face of an ax. Would that be the flat? No. The face of an ax is the sharp line. The dividing line, the line that makes section. It is not a face at all.

Ariel Price thinks on this, because it is painfully relevant. The room into which he has been thrown—following the fire, following the judgment—has no floor. It has walls, yes, a wall to either side, but these walls meet at a linear seam beneath his feet. It is not a floor at all.

A room like an ax. "You can kill a person as easily with a room as with an ax." Who had said that? Some Romantic poet from the fatherland. Silly, Ariel had thought in school. Meaningless. How could a room be like an ax? But now he is here.

It is not clear that the cell is intended to kill him, but it is certainly uncomfortable.

He draws the space in his mind. The section: two lines meeting sharply at the lowest point. He extrudes this space laterally from the section, and produces—what?—a space like a partially opened book. A book opened upward to the sky. Two segments of line that meet at a vertex become, in the three-dimensional mind, two planes that meet in a seam.

Ariel lifts himself up from where he was thrown, and works to orient himself in the cell. He puts a foot on either wall; that is too difficult; it bends the aged ankles. He tries to wedge one foot into the sharp angle where the walls meet beneath him, but that too is painful. At last he determines that he is most comfortable with his back against one wall, and his feet against the other. His knees push up against his chest.

This is not painful, but humiliating.

A perfect four-sided hole is dug into the earth on the mount, equidistant from either thief. Four straight sides of rough earth, and the space between them, expectant. Punishment is spatial. The cross, nailed to the man, is carried roughly through the dirt by soldiers. The cross and man emerge into the frame of our vision—the proscenium arch, the frame of history—foreshortened, the body long with suffering.

The crucifixion is only the beginning.

A deep rectangular prism, air bounded by earth, awaits the cross. Two beams, rough-hewn and nailed perpendicular, ordinary trees, undergo with this emergence into the frame of history—rendered in exaggerated perspective down through the flaking pigment of centuries—a transformation. They become The Cross: the structure of punishment iconic and perfect, so that two scraped lines in a mud wall will mean forever this: eternal suffering, the architecture of pain.

Growing in our vision as it approaches through the frame of history, the foot of the cross makes its way, imperfectly, toward the four-sided hole. Skulls crunch and split beneath the feet of soldiers. The man on the cross groans, soft delirious words, lambent Aramaic.

Only the beginning.

The cross is tipped, the base—square in plan—edged toward the square hole. The man, his frame sagging on the upward-tilting spine of the cross, cries out, his cry stopped by the new and unnatural pressure on his lungs, his body so twisted and heavy. As the body of the man sinks, spread between nails, two thousand years of painters and sculptors move feverishly in sleep, waiting. A collective groan.

In the beginning was the empty space, expectant.

The beam slides roughly into its waiting hole, and with an audible thud meets earth. The man, hung vertically now, can barely breathe. His skin is wet with suffering and blood. The soldiers, their task complete, are still uneasy. One of them begins to cry, softly.

To either side, a thief changes. A terrible, beautiful calm descends upon each, and his private sky is washed in morning light. Hands pierced and bleeding, feet shattered and twisted to the side, lungs almost flattened between wrenched bones, each thief achieves, for the first time in a misery-soaked life—and until the last bell rings life into the bone-dry ears of the waiting dead—ecstasy.

Ariel hangs there, fetal, suspended above the floor that is not a floor, and thinks hard about judgment. Clearly, an architect has designed this cell: it is with some anger and a sense of betrayal that Ariel comes to this conclusion. No engineer would have the sense to punish him in this way. Irony is the province of architects and poets: somebody is watching him.

And with this thought, he knows that it is true. He is being watched. He puts his hand to his forehead, the translucent skin above and between the eyes, and tries to massage away this sensation: that he is being watched. The pineal gland, once the hook into the soul—the Cartesian universal joint by which the spinning of the soul turned the wheels of the flesh—is much less now, in an age of medicine and method, but it is something. It is here, in the crippled vestigial organ between the eyes, that the body finds its daily rhythm of sleep and wakefulness in concert with the sun. The circadian rhythm. Something like the old cosmological dance to the tune of the spheres, but considerably reduced. Mundane. As much like the ancient harmonies as this—the withered organ beneath the brow—is kin to the glittering eye.

Yet Ariel Price has always known about the pineal gland: that it has a sense unique to it. Hold a finger half an inch from the center of the forehead, and although the eyes are closed, you sense that a finger is there. Ariel knows this. And this is the organ that says to the architect: you are being watched.

He can see almost nothing himself. It is clear that the room—

Can you call a space without a floor a room?—is long, much longer than he can see from here, from the entrance. It is dim in the cell, and the two walls seem to extend inward a great distance. By shuffling along the wedge—moving first his spine a few inches, then his feet—Ariel can make progress into the darkness. Awkward, graceless progress. It is deeply humiliating.

He makes his way.

The guard had been ax-faced.

The door had shut with the sound of a guillotine.

The plan for the cell had issued, with blood, from a paper cut.

Jernigan labors over a sheet of Mylar. He applies the hypodermic tip of the technical pen to the perfect surface, as if injecting a clean drug into the upper layer of skin, or applying a tattoo. Leaving the needle tip, the ink spreads into a raised line, precise in width and consistency: the memory of the hand's guided passage.

Jernigan is particular about his equipment. The drafting table is pine, the angle of the surface adjusted by tightening bolts that pass through semicircular rails. His pens, tipped with jewels, are sleek and aerodynamic, a science fiction, as if designed for interplanetary travel. And in truth, they do effect a passage: from the harrowed intricate mind of the unknown architect into the diagrammatic garden of lines from which will flower the perfect prison. Jernigan's hands are the medium between worlds: the precise mechanical means of reproduction, through which thought becomes matter. The philosopher's hinge, the pineal gland.

The drawings are themselves remarkable. A line scratched on film often is. The workers who handle the drawings of Jernigan Noer are shamed into perfection; they know that the thought made line will never survive the transition to steel and stone without an admixture of error.

The design has come a great distance from Stein Foregutt's whimsical pronouncement upon an accident with a piece of paper: Jernigan has perfected, mentally, the architecture of punishment.

As he makes his careful way toward the inner cell, Ariel Price discerns in the darkness the unsettling features of his new home. The seam where the walls meet is not level with the ground plane; this requires him to edge his way up as well as along. And the fold is complex: his journey is not a straight line. The walls change direction, ever so slightly, requiring him to reposition his body every time he meets one of these subtle corners. The effect is distressing: it indicates to the architect that his cell is not geometrically simple, and thus not entirely knowable in the dark, and thus, perhaps, capable of offering at any moment a truly rude surprise.

Ariel prefers Cartesian space. We know this. Extrusions from a grid. They appeal to the ordering will, such spaces. The subtle corner is a monstrosity. The "skew." Loathsome. It suggests that the grid lacks authority, that nature contributes something irrational to subvert genius, that Ariel and his peers (of which there are few) are not omnipotent. Whoever planned the line of his floor has a devious and decadent mind. He is a true enemy.

Yes, whoever designed the cell knows what it is that Ariel requires, spatially, and chose very carefully to deny it. Not simply to deny, but to refute it. In a manner too subtle to suggest that Ariel, in his life practice, was wholly wrong—simply to suggest that Ariel's truth was only partial, and perhaps shallow.

There may well be a grid, says this invisible architect in his prison design, but life always manages to elude it. Even your life, Ariel Price. Your life, and its sentence.

The great architect seethes.

How do they plan these buildings, he wonders. What kind of drawing—say, a traditional cut at knee-level—could possibly describe this: a room without a floor, whose walls make a mockery of Euclid? He wonders about this decadent practice, and surprises himself as he begins to yield to grudging admiration: it cannot be easy. Quickly, however, the brooding critic returns to reason: years of paring down, decades of refinement, have created something finally unyielding in Ariel Price. A sense of what is permissible. This cell is the work of an evil and unprincipled mind.

He inches along, increasingly affronted by each almost imperceptible change in direction, and feels forward with his right hand into the darkness.

He is climbing, apparently, toward an event.

A cross awaits at the top of the hill that Ariel's taxi climbs. Lit with garish lights, and raised beside a pitchfork-like antenna, the cross beams out across the city of Montreal, its proportions unchanged from those two hacked beams of wood.

Ariel will not ascend the Mountain, not today: he has an appointment with another man, beneath the eye of the cross, on a street called Esplanade. In an old striped house, four stories high, Theseus Crouch gathering notes and scraps of a life awaits the architect's footstep.

Beneath the humming tires, the road is as smooth as a skull. The taxi ascends to the Plateau.

Cosimo details the inner room. It will be a four-sided space at the center of the mall: four perfect black walls holding a prism of unlit air. Cosimo has surrounded his drafting table with images of the crucifixion. On each he has drawn, in red ink, a circle: identifying the place at which the base of the cross meets the earth of Golgotha. Cosimo has rendered hundreds of careful drawings, rectangular prisms, the space of the hole in the earth occupied by the end of that square beam.

In his mind, Cosimo has enlarged that hole into a raging abyss.

And it is this that he creates for Ariel Price, his malevolent mentor: an empty space, magnified and darkened, at the center of the foundations, its proportions perfect for the insertion of a giant, impossible crucifix.

Ariel Price sits hunched in gloom over his long, long desk. He does not look up as Cosimo enters the room. He examines the marbled surface of the desk, how the gloom contains within it enough light to illuminate small flaws in the surface. Hell is in the details.

"Sir?"

Ariel looks up, annoyed.

"You, um, you asked me to come up?"

With a visible effort, Ariel smiles.

"Yes. Yes, I did. Are you finished?"

"I think so. I . . . I have a set of drawings . . . I think they're pretty good."

"Good."

In the long uncomfortable silence that ensues, Cosimo edges closer to the desk.

"Sir?"

Again, Ariel's features register irritation: What is it?

"Sir, I . . . think it's a good room. I mean, as an exercise in proportion and detail. It's very . . . simple. Very beautiful. I've stripped away everything but the essence. It's a . . . perfect room, I think."

"Good."

"And, uh . . . I was wondering . . . I mean, I know that function doesn't really matter to you, and uh, we've never discussed program, but . . ."

"Hm?"

"I was just wondering . . ."

In the silence, Cosimo's eyes began to adjust to the murk.

"Sir?"

Cosimo can make out the tension, raising lines in the back of the great, clawlike hands.

"Sir, what's it for?"

Ariel smiles again. A genuine smile, this time. "That's why you're here."

Cosimo and Bethany sit in a tiny coffee shop on College Street. Still nervous in her presence, Cosimo touches her hands and then retreats as if in pain.

"I don't know what to say, Bethany. I don't trust him. I don't like him. But he asked me to speak to you, and it's your decision . . ."

"Why would he want me to perform?"

"I don't know. He watched you dancing in the square and he . . . he thought you were good. He was 'captivated.' That's the word he used. 'Captivated.' "

191

Bethany grimaces. "I really don't like to think he's been . . . watching me this whole time. It makes everything feel disgusting, as if I've been . . ."

Cosimo touched her hand to silence the thought.

"I wasn't dancing for him."

"I know. But he was there. Anyway you can just decline, you know. You don't owe him anything."

"But you work for him. Isn't it going to get you in trouble?"

"This isn't about me."

"What's the harm in just putting on a performance? It's kind of an opportunity. I mean, he's famous . . ."

"He's a fraud."

"But he's famous. An important person. If he likes my dancing, you know, maybe he can help me."

"Help you do what?"

"I don't know. I don't know."

Cosimo was unhappy that he had broached the topic. "Just decline, Bethany. It's an old man having weird fantasies; it's meaningless; it's not going to help your career."

Bethany was silent. She blew on her coffee, then took a careful sip.

"Bethany . . ."

"Nobody's ever asked me to dance for them before."

"I don't trust him."

". . . and it's a big deal, being asked to augurate . . ."

"Inaugurate."

"Whatever. Being asked to do that."

"For what? Being asked to inaugurate a windowless room in the basement of a tower? It's just weird."

Bethany smiled. "You designed it, Cosimo."

Cosimo, reddening, dipped a finger in his coffee and sucked on it.

"You designed it. It's your first built piece. Let me do this for you. I'll dance for you."

Cosimo could not speak.

"I want to do it, Cosimo."

A line of shadowy souls moves graveward, not yet to die but to witness. What becomes later enacted as the race to the grave is in truth a movement painfully slow, a performance of Zeno's paradox, for motion is impossible. He is dead.

Always, when we arrive at that empty tomb, Saintes-Maries is there ahead of us. None of us has fallen far enough to be first to be raised; she is there ahead of us. Our sins are banal; her sin uniquely an excess of virtue. She loved too many. She was too much inclined toward love. We were fishermen failing in the simple command to love our vile neighbors, and she was already there giving comfort to lepers and syphilitic footmen. Always already there.

The audience below, watching the great architect in his cage, is made nervous by the monstrous wedge suspended above them. It seems perpetually in the condition of descent; it hangs, indecently, from an irrational array of beams—as if toothpicks had been scattered on the floor, and this pattern had been faithfully copied in the lattice of beams that pierces the great knife-like object, holding it in place like a wedge of lemon at the mouth of a glass.

Those who know anything of Ariel Price ponder the first of the "five points" much discussed by his friend the Vulture at Deux Magots: the *Pilotis*, thin vertical pillars, cylindrical, to raise the mass of the house above the ground plane. This chaos of beams is a mockery.

As Ariel Price makes his way along the crease in his cell, the audience watches, slightly ashamed. It does not seem decent to watch greatness, however fallen, tortured in this way. That Herr Price can be seen but cannot see inspires the audience with a sense of their own prurience: they are voyeurs, and this punishment is, in many ways, pornographic. Dignity rendered ridiculous: perhaps the essence of pornography.

And, of course, there are the cameras.

Every movement of the great man is monitored, enlarged, and displayed for the nervous audience, who know that Price himself cannot see this.

The fourth of the five points—the Horizontal Sliding Window—is now this: a silent camera, invisible, which pans the length of the cell and makes a window of his progress.

An optical nerve that culminates in an opaque surface. The pineal gland. This is what Ariel Price senses: somewhere in his cell—perhaps everywhere—there are optical nerves that end darkly, much as the third eye in the center of his forehead ends not in a lens, but papery skin. Blindness that sees. It is appalling.

He makes his way, and is watched. The Free Plan, the second of the five points (even Ariel Price is aware of the mockery now) has been pulled almost straight, stretched like a dead snake into a rough line. His uncomfortable movement is tracing the line of an architectural satire.

Ariel's discomfort grows with every awkward wriggle. He feels, increasingly, that he is squirming in a jar for the pleasure of children, that every indignation to which he is subjected is not simply for his experience—as punishment—but exists for some other, wholly repulsive reason: perhaps for entertainment.

He cannot imagine that he has become the stuff of entertainment. Everything that he has done in life—his work, his crime, *especially* his recent crime—has been done for this reason: so that he might be taken seriously. The biography of a great man, for Ariel Price, is an abomination: an opportunity for peons to open the book of greatness and leaf through it as if it were a salacious magazine. And that is why his own biographer had to be deemed the enemy. There is no indignity worse than the intimate put on display.

And he thinks on the fifth point: the Roof Garden. The surreal masque—a substitute for the displaced garden below—placed high and on display, an entertainment for the eyes. He has become a roof garden.

He has accustomed himself now to the almost-darkness, and he can make out, spanning the space above him, the chaos of beams that pierces the cell and holds it aloft.

The handle of the ax.

The door to the cell had a great handle.

The judge had pointed with the handle of his gavel: "Life."

Every ax, to become a tool, must solve the point of nexus: blade and handle.

As the architectural team works in electronic space to position the axlike cell, an engineer calculates the weight. "It is not very efficient to hang a room from I-beams, you know." The architect silences him with a pitying glance. Yes, yes, I know, thinks the engineer: efficiency is passé. Bloody architects.

Stein Foregutt and his most digitally adept employee—the one whose fingers fly over the keyboard with musical precision—are turning the great ax in the non-space of the monitor. Jernigan Noer has proved uncannily proficient with the most sophisticated tools. Three dimensions, rendered increasingly clear with each subtle turn. The great French sculptor had worked like this: profile, turn, profile, turn . . . Until the statue was complete. Difficult objects require difficult methods: to each thing its requisite complexity. Elegance grows out of chaos.

To increase disorder: that is the goal. The cosmos presents us with a measure of chaos, and the human mind is naturally inclined to work against this. Only the truly ambitious mind would think to *add* to this. To add to the mess.

It was a fit punishment for the man who had thought only in perfect rectangles. The team pushed at his famous grid until it came subtly apart at the seams, then made a seam that suggested this: the binding together of the broken in permanent brokenness. And hung that emblem high. Ariel Price, they knew, would hate it with his whole being.

This was the penultimate decision. To elevate the cell high above the audience, to hang it there like judgment itself: sharp and potent, energy stored perhaps for centuries until the earth shifts, the beams break, and the great ax comes down. A physicist much loved by architects had been moved in his autobiography by the fact of latent energy: every stone raised by the mason has the potential to come down eventually causing death. The conservation of energy.

The last decision, the one that makes sense of them all, has yet to be experienced by Ariel Price.

Price edges his way along the bending seam, and ponders the mockery. Five points.

He thinks back on those afternoons in the cafe, with the Vulture, when they would plan the razing of Paris. Nothing in his life had come close to the pleasure of those discussions. Free and open conversation between men of genius. The greatest pleasure. And my, how they had dressed in those days: the long coats, the sculpted eyeglass frames; they had been like gods.

The ridges of his spine ache where they abrade against the wall behind him.

The cell is filling now with distant light, a grim light from on deep.

He makes his way toward it, edging painfully, wondering.

The Free Facade: Have they forgotten one of the five?

Fools. They have forgotten the principles.

The team waited as the architect rolled his pencil back and forth along the table, thinking in silence. What would it be? What would it be? A man who would erase his own biography deserves what? And how would they implement the last of the five points (third, in theory): the Free Facade, the elevation independent of structure, purely sculptural, an echo of the freedom of the plan?

How would they turn this freedom into a prison?

The light grows.

The taxi bearing Ariel Price turns onto rue Esplanade. Theseus Crouch, sweating in his only suit, has developed a rash on his plump wrists. He shifts his watch to relieve the inflamed skin: any moment the great man will arrive.

Theseus is determined not to be sycophantic. He knows his natural impulse in the presence of the famous, his tendency to emphasize his practiced English accent and to fall into a pattern of false familiarity—just you and me, we know how it is, I was at Cambridge actually—but this famous man, now approaching, is a criminal. Theseus, with a tremendous effort of will, curbs his impulse toward awe. Heel.

Ariel emerges from the cab. He pays the driver with crisp candy-colored bills, and takes his change in the cheap metal coin of the realm.

The street into which he emerges leaves him disoriented. It is only half a street. On the one side, a row of those peculiar houses, ironwork circulation hanging from the facade like a man with his lungs coughed out; on the other a darkened park rising toward a cross of bright lights, almost surreal in its attitude toward faith and taste. Where am I, thinks this adrenalated architect: Is this a city?

The soundtrack to a Western drifts out from an open window, crackling with layers of media static: analog hiss, broken transmission, cultural confusion. The blue light of a television rises and falls, uneasy ghost, and the soundtrack sings thinly. Ariel shivers in the vulgar air.

Theseus Crouch hovers spiderlike behind his window, waiting with glowing agitation for the arrival of his protagonist. Despite his academic poverty, Crouch has a sumptuous apartment, with two capacious rooms and an impressive kitchen. He has a balcony. He has a view of the park. This is Montreal, where even third-rate biographers live like royalty. Surely he will not stand me up? Theseus Crouch adjusts his bulging vest and traces the insides of his red lips with an anxious tongue.

Ariel swings the iron gate.

The moment is sick with imprecise drama. The predator spies his predator. They gaze upon each other. Simultaneously, with a thrill of fear and malevolence, each is aware of the other's presence. The seeing, despite the biographer's cowardly stance at the window, is mutual.

Price.

Crouch.

Do I meet him at the door, wonders Theseus Crouch, unnerved at the moment of recognition. We are both aware that we here: Which would betray coarseness, cowardice? To wait for a ring, or to preempt it? I have been seen, after all.

In the end, Theseus Crouch miscalculates. He decides to intercept the architect at the entrance, but Price arrives at the glass door in time to see the fat biographer waddling nervously down the interior stair, practicing his suave greeting to the air.

When he views the hideous wraith staring up at him with unconcealed disdain, the biographer stumbles.

Ariel waits.

With painful awkwardness, Theseus Crouch attempts to descend. Despite his effort to slow his movement, he seems to scurry, rodentlike, to greet his subject.

Ariel waits.

Theseus Crouch arrives panting at the door. He opens it with the caricature of a sly smile, "Herr Price, I assume."

Idiot. Idiot! Why did I have to say that? "Herr Price, I assume." Fool! That is not clever.

Price says nothing. Less being more.

Saintes-Maries, weeping as if her eyes have only so many hours of weeping left before they are cut out—and they have—feels a voice at her shoulder.

"It hurts me to see my most dearly beloved so unhappy. I have taken your pain upon me for today. Be happy, Mary."

"Teacher . . ."

"You have loved more greatly than any, Mary. You alone have made me ashamed of my love. Even dying for their sins, I have not offered myself as completely as you. Be happy, Mary, for in falling most low you have risen most high."

Mary turns to the ghost at her shoulder, and seeing him, reaches out.

"No! Do not touch me." The ghost is crying.

Mary sinks back into her sorrow, cut to the spine.

"I am so sorry, Mary. I cannot save you any of the pain that awaits you. But be happy today. I am with you."

The angels sweep the grave, bored.

"Will you walk with me, Mary?"

A DIALOGUE BETWEEN
THE BIOGRAPHER AND THE ARCHITECT

PRICE:
You live well. For a member of the academy.

CROUCH:
The physical environment has always been of the utmost importance to me.

PRICE:
Hence the study of architecture.

CROUCH:
I am very sensitive to my surroundings.

PRICE:
You look like a very sensitive man.

CROUCH:
Um, yes. Thank you.

PRICE:
Tell me. Where are you from, Mr. Crouch? Your accent.

CROUCH:
England, actually. My accent . . . well, it's a Cambridge accent.
Not really so much a regional as a college pretense.

*THESEUS CROUCH laughs, too informally, too
loudly.*

PRICE:
And your . . . region?

A long silence.

PRICE:
Never mind. The English and . . . my people. We share a
commonality of purpose. A culture. Don't we. I greatly
admire certain English architects.

CROUCH:
Oh really? Which ones?

ARIEL PRICE is at a loss to name a single English architect that he admires.

PRICE:
The . . . the names escape me at the moment. But we share a language, almost: a blood, a history. We are cultured people. Why are you writing this book?

THESEUS CROUCH busies himself in the kitchen.

CROUCH:
Can I offer you some sherry?

PRICE:
No, thank you.

CROUCH:
Some crackers with cheese?

PRICE:
No, thank you.

CROUCH:
You don't mind if I have a little snack.

PRICE:
Please. Go ahead. Mr. Crouch, why are you writing this book?
I am a serious man.

THESEUS CROUCH emerges with crackers on a tray.
He has a small piece of cheese clinging to the underside
of his cherubic lip.

CROUCH:

I too am a serious man, Mr. Price. You do not know of me,
but we serious men sometimes labor in obscurity. I have
labored in obscurity, Herr Price. I fully expect this biography
to change all that. Biographers are much admired these days.

PRICE:

Is it the money? I can assure you that the biography of an
architect will not make you wealthy. You live well, Mr.
Crouch, but I could perhaps arrange it so that you lived
somewhat better.

CROUCH:
I, well . . .

PRICE:

Now, I'll be honest with you, Mr. Crouch. I am not a rich
man. But I am willing to make a profound personal sacrifice
to prevent your ill-advised treatise from confusing future
biographers. I could afford a sum of say, ten thousand dollars.
A kill fee, if you like.

CROUCH:
Mr. Price, I don't believe you understand my motivation.

PRICE:
I do not.

CROUCH:
I am a man of principle, Mr. Price. A man, dare I say it, very
like the man you are commonly thought to be. A man of the
highest principles. I am concerned with truth. Truth, beauty
and justice.

PRICE:
Ah. As in the comic books.

CROUCH:
I do not read comic books, sir.

PRICE:
What region of London did you say you hailed from again?
Oh, you did not. I'm not very good with accents, I'm afraid.
But yours sounds almost proletarian.

*THESEUS CROUCH, purple with indignation, chokes
on a cracker.*

PRICE:
Would that be the manuscript in question?

*ARIEL PRICE steps toward the desk in the corner, on
which is stacked a tall pile of ragged papers. Crouch,
moving with the swiftness of a crab, interposes himself
between the architect and the desk.*

CROUCH:
Sir. That would be the manuscript. I am sorry if I cannot
permit you to peruse it at the moment.

PRICE:
How unfortunate. I would love to read about myself. No
doubt you have tremendous insights.

CROUCH:
I have been told that I do, yes.

PRICE:
That must be very gratifying.

The conversation itself becomes immaterial from this point.
Any text may be substituted. Pleasantries bordering on insults
may be suggested through dance, ambient tape loops, projection. Growing in focus and importance, however, is the manuscript lying informally, pregnant, a fat odalisque, on the
biographer's desk.

The center of Ariel Price's vision has been usurped by this
manuscript, evil and insistent, on the periphery. Although his
eyes are fixed on the portly figure of Theseus Crouch, the booming, buzzing edges of his hemisphere of vision are alive with the
fact of these menacing pages.

They grow. The apartment dims. Theseus Crouch dimin-
ishes in the great man's sight until he is an insect; Price could
reach and press him between two fingers like this. But the pages
grow. They grow and fester, slippery with ink, interleaving. Ariel
Price can smell the pages from across the room. The stench of
festering paper. Rats scurry between the pages, brushing against
words. The title page laughs with psychotic abandon and ex-
poses itself to the audience. A footnote screams. More laughter.
Ariel Price, sickening visibly, his eyes again growing wild, ex-
cuses himself from the presence of the biographer to disappear

into the trees across the road, which open to swallow him and give him animal shelter, the great mind seething. Night falls.

The hours spent in that dense wooded park with copulating thieves and midnight joggers is best left undescribed. Ariel Price, returned from the lowest place on earth, descends. Drums boom dimly from the shadows, gathering terrible force and sending pebbles cascading from the path. Ariel Price crouched feral over a dark object—description is best left unexplored—gnaws on his lips until they bleed. An uneasy moon, gibbous, scuttles frightened between the skeletal trees. Price tastes the soil and howls.

Theseus Crouch, shaken but pleased with himself, spreads cheese on a thin bagel.

A MEETING OF WHORES

"Will you walk with me, Mary?" Yes. Yes, I will.

Mary touches her eyelids, which flutter wet beneath her fingers. She can feel the spherical organs of sight move beneath the closed lids, and for a moment she stands like this, giving thanks for the fact and the apparatus of vision.

When she opens her eyes, her teacher is still standing at her shoulder. "Do you doubt that it is me?"

No. No, I have no doubt.

"Come walk."

Saintes-Maries follows her risen teacher as he makes his way down the small mountain. She turns briefly to look back at the crucifix, but it has changed. Where once it was square timbers roughly nailed and drenched in blood, now it is festooned in garish lights. An angel, bored, in a blue polyester shirt with a name sewn over the left breast pocket, changes a lightbulb. Two centurions jog by, wearing Nikes.

Saintes-Maries and her teacher make their way down Mont Royal to the plateau.

In the wild places off the path an old man with lupine hair finds love with a young Québecoise. She, incoherent with youth and an impure substance licked from the surface of a tambourine, closes her eyes and barely winces as the architect enters her from behind. Fingering her beads, Ariel Price lets out a guttural ululation as the drums roar. After decades of strict discipline, Price permits his potent seed to enter the public sphere.

As the architect emerges from the underbrush, wiping his hands on his trousers, he comes face to face with a young woman of haggard but undeniable beauty. Startled, the architect reverts to German. Uncomprehending, the young woman answers in Aramaic, which the architect mistakes for French. He does not notice the figure standing behind her in the shadows, bleeding from terrible wounds in the hands and feet. After a few moments of failed conversation, the young woman smiles, touches him on the shoulder, and passes on.

With that touch, Ariel Price is filled with the excruciating recognition of freedom. He can turn back. The path reveals a fork, and he need not pursue his terrible course into the night: anything is possible, even redemption. He does not know why he knows this, but this woman has fallen lower than even he, greatest whore of his time and profession, has fallen; and yet she has been redeemed.

Turn back.

Reader, lay this book aside. You do not wish to follow Ariel

Price in his chosen path. You too have been offered a nexus, a numinous branching path toward something less horrible than what this night has in store. Lay this book aside and follow that young woman in your mind, for we shall not meet her again within these pages. Between whores, choose the one who is saved.

You will not? I take no responsibility for your soul.

We go with Ariel Price, then, the architect with the stained trousers; we follow him down the tiny urban mountain as he makes his purposed way toward rue Esplanade. In his pocket, a book of matches stolen from the filthy girl who sleeps now, aching in her dreams, against a rotting tree.

We return to Tom Sorrow, descending alone the swift elevator. It is late. His characteristic smile, even when alone, has faded, and lines of care have written themselves into his young skin. The terrible fact can no longer be ignored: he is losing staff at an appalling rate. Secretaries and office boys, evaporating into the public space like mist, and never a trace. Tom has not known any of them long enough to develop an attachment, but the simple matter of constant flux is enough to derail the simple trainlike path of his mind. To deviate the plow from its furrow. Tom has never known complexity before. He brushed against it once, in his encounters with Scilla and her friends, but he never properly understood: even the cleanest landscape, even the most pristine structure cannot preserve the virginity of line deep into the foundation.

The tiny room descends on its cable.

No, every line when followed to the source will reveal something terribly nonlinear, incapable of rule. Tom has fooled himself these many years into the false belief that things persist, that order underlies, but the secretaries have vanished.

In front of him, the line of buttons indicates with precision the placement of floors. A counter over his head triangulates: this moving room is now aligned specifically at the nexus between the central shaft and the seventh floor. On the brushed steel panel in front of him, the buttons march.

Descent is painfully slow today.

The final button, marked with an L, is lit from the pressure of Tom's finger. To descend into the mall, a passenger is required to exit from the tiny room into the cathedral lobby, and from there ride a cycling escalator into the subcity.

Tom traces the line of buttons with his index finger, letting the fingertip rest on the steel plate an inch below the lit L. He closes his eyes, distracted. The elevator is slow today. The steel beneath his finger grows warm.

Tom opens his eyes to find that the fingernail on his index finger is growing, perceptibly, as it rests against the plate. He pulls it back, in disgust, to reveal a nascent button, fetal and strange, where before there was only the blankness of brushed steel. This button, emerging below the pale L, glows.

The doors open into the lobby, briefly admitting the night. Tom does not move. The doors close, and the tiny room descends.

Ariel's knifelike room opens into light: a sharp triangular wall of glass looking out and down upon the audience.

Yes, there is an audience. Dressed mostly in black, with aggressively tailored clothes and serious expressions, they are clearly design students. And when Ariel Price makes his appearance, like a fly on the windshield above, they clap appreciatively.

This in itself is not horrifying. Price has trained himself, through years of ascetic arrogance, to disregard the sheeplike movements of students and young designers, and that they are now here, toasting him in his prison with a polite ovation and highballs raised, is of no particular concern.

The wall opposite, however, is appalling.

Whoever has designed this prison has worked out a punishment beyond architecture. (Or so Price thinks: his narrow view of what constitutes "architecture" is incapable of including the horror opposite, although one man—the mysterious Jernigan Noer—considers this aspect of the design, if anything, the quintessence of architecture.)

The wall is endless. Freestanding, leaning away from the cell window, and apparently without end: it disappears into the sky above with the pretense to infinity that is the hallmark of a Price tower. But this is no tower.

Nor is it, strictly speaking, a wall. It is a page. A white expanse, across whose surface dances an electronic array of letters. Transfixed by the vile ingenuity of his prison designer—Stein Foregutt would claim authorship, of course, but this is entirely the child of Jernigan Noer—the prisoner, despite himself, begins to read.

Ariel Price stands in the street, contemplating the unseasonable warmth—warm enough for an encounter in the midnight park—and weighs the small can in his papery hand. Although bent on a linear task, Ariel Price has allowed himself a small detour to the corner for a can of lighter fluid. Growing delirious, he again deviates from his pursuit, five times, to purchase five more slim containers.

He returns a sixth time to purchase a large can of barbecue

starter. The man behind the cash register stares at him with growing distrust. When Ariel Price departs this last time, the cashier stands in the doorway and watches as the architect makes a determined line down rue Esplanade.

Theseus Crouch is reposed in a vinyl recliner, wearing headphones; he is listening to the Hallelujah Chorus of Handel's *Messiah*, his favorite piece of music. The king may stand for this chorus, but not Theseus Crouch. He sits back in his chair, with his eyes closed, nibbling on a croissant slathered with butter. Well. The great man has tried to purchase the integrity of Theseus Crouch, but the biographer has demonstrated his superiority, proved his human worth, by resisting the base offer. And Theseus, I assure you, would know what to do with ten thousand dollars: he is a creature of refined taste.

While it is true that Theseus Crouch is not a religious man, he has nevertheless developed a voyeur's appreciation for the religious aesthetic. He enjoys Sunday Mass. He has made friends with powerful clerics and discussed elements of the ritual with them; Theseus Crouch, although he failed Latin, vastly prefers the Latin Mass for its purity and consistency with the great line of tradition. The architect's offensive suggestion, that Theseus Crouch has not fully overcome his suburban origins, is a mark of ignorance: if Ariel Price could see the biographer enjoying his *Messiah* and his croissant, he would be convinced otherwise.

But Ariel Price cannot see this. He is not far from the plump reclining figure, but he cannot see Theseus Crouch. For the architect is intent upon the task at hand.

Tom's elevator descends into the rectangular prison of air that waits. Cosimo Neri had designed the base of the elevator shaft as if it were a foundation itself, and the shaft an armless crucifix. Tom's tiny room fits into this perfect hole with a silent but perceptible thud. The doors do not open. But the mirrored walls of the elevator begin to admit something more than reflection.

Ariel Price slipped through the front door of the building behind Crouch's upstairs neighbor, who carried groceries and had no reason to distrust the thin, dignified man. Price held the door for her, smiling, then followed her into the hall. Now he stands outside Theseus Crouch's door, where he squeezes a thin yellow can, sending irregular streams of vaporous liquid through the slot between the bottom of the door and the painted threshold. The biographer, immersed now in Pachelbel's *Canon*, flares his nostrils and twitches: some fool is preparing a barbecue on a balcony in the middle of winter.

Tom's elevator walls accumulate transparency as dim light illuminates the obverse side of the mirrors. He is standing in an increasingly undefined cage, a disappearing box, and about him the visible space is vast. Flickering about him, alive in the wild expanse of the mall, are dim fires. He places a hand against the mirror in front of him—all of his fingernails are longer now, and curling to the side—and it feels nothing but air. Tom Sorrow steps through the wall of his elevator into the welcoming gloom of the subcity.

When the fifth can of lighter fluid has been emptied beneath the door, Ariel begins to pour the barbecue starter. The odor is intoxicating. Theseus Crouch, who has raised himself from his repose to switch Pachelbel for his beloved Barber *Adagio*, can no longer ignore the pungency of the great pool spreading through his living room. Good god: the floor is wet!

The growing toxic puddle is licking the soles of his wing tips. Theseus steps back in alarm, but the floor behind him is also slick with liquid. Ariel stands back from his accomplishment, lights a wooden match, and tosses it with a flourish toward the crack beneath the door.

Theseus hears the spark of the match, its voracious consumption of sulfur, and he knows. Screaming, he stumbles backward but falls in his haste, soaking his good suit in the rear, and with a low sound as if his apartment has become a throat and is inhaling flame, the wooden floor becomes an instant conflagration, Theseus Crouch merely one crying topographical extremity in a map of fire.

Ariel Price hears the dragon's breath as he moves swiftly down the stairs and into the street. He does not look back, but the flames cast his shadow long in front of him. The agonized howl of Theseus Crouch is deeply satisfying. Ariel makes his way into the madness of the moon-drenched park.

On the glowing desk, papers turn as they curl in flame. Theseus Crouch, screaming on the floor, will never see again, but were his streaming eyes still organs of sight he might read the following—words that he himself has written—before they disappear into the roaring, all-consuming air.

THE STRUCTURE OF PUNISHMENT

What is surprising, again and again, is how disingenuous the great man's allegiance really is to the aes-

thetics of tallness. Ariel Price, who made the city tall, never really had any plan to accomplish this. The bitter truth is that throughout his life he preferred the horizontal. If you were to ask Price why he considered the Letztesmann Tower a masterpiece, the answer would probably not much accord with the critics' consensus: it would have nothing to do with the proportions of the great elevator shaft, the mock-structural detailing of the curtain wall, the massing of pink travertine in the lobby; no, I feel certain that Ariel Price's obsession, and greatest secret, is the creation of the growing insatiable maze, the mall beneath the street that gradually comes to undermine the foundation of the central downtown core, the creeping rot that Ariel Price bequeathed to the solid earth of the New World.

Little has been written about the inner chamber. It is assumed never to have been built, since it has never been found. And yet it exists in the final plan: a room, detailed in his assistant's hand, directly beneath the shaft of the central elevator. I have spent time in the mall beneath the Letztesmann Tower; I have mapped that place using a compass and string, and I can tell you this: there is indeed a space that cannot be entered, immediately beneath the central elevator. It has no door. It has therefore never been discovered. And yet it is there: my calculations demonstrated to me that it must be there, just as it appears in the drawing.

I was determined to investigate the purpose of this blind room, and although I understood that the Letztesmann Tower is considered a landmark building, and is protected, I imagine my readers will sympathize with the overwhelming urge toward the truth which caused me to begin, surreptitiously, my own midnight excavation into the mystery of that hollow foundation. My discovery is nothing less than the greatest architectural revelation of our day.

Cosimo took Bethany by the wet hand, and led her down into the reaches beneath the growing tower. He flashed an identity card at the bored watchman who guarded the inner building site, and passed into the unfinished mall.

"Is it far?" Bethany was shivering.

"Sort of. Right at the center. It's a bit complex, finding it, but I drew this place; I know the way. Are you sure you want to go through with this?"

"I'm sure."

They continued.

"And . . . where is he?"

"Waiting for us. He is there."

For a long time they walked in silence.

"We can always turn back."

"No, this is important. I want to do it."

Cosimo sighed. They stepped through the darkness.

Although we associate Ariel Price with his dramatic yet destructive influence on the urban skyline, he has admitted more than once that his decision to build tall was dictated entirely by clients and market forces. The architect, he reminds us, is a whore. And if a good whore is asked to perform a service, he will bend to the task without complaining. The Price clients wanted tall buildings. Ariel aimed to please. And yes, he concocted

*the lie regarding his adolescent dream; but more than
once he slipped and denied it: Ariel Price had no personal allegiance to the tall.*

*Which is not to say that the whore did not preserve,
deep within himself, his own cherished notions. I have
called attention before to the Price impulse toward
depth; it was only through my careful excavation of the
Letztesmann mall that I was to discover the piteous
extremes to which that thwarted impulse would move
him. Ariel Price, whore, remained in his mind an ardent lover.*

"I won't be able to stay with you."

Bethany turned to Cosimo, suddenly frightened. "Why
not?"

"He doesn't want me. He . . . told me. You're supposed to
dance just for him."

"Cosimo . . ."

"You don't have to."

Bethany stopped moving. She was wavering. "I don't understand this."

"I'm not sure he can be understood. He's a strange man."

She touched Cosimo's face, and as always he shut his eyes
in a vain effort to prevent her sight. Don't look at me. They
stood beneath construction lights: bare bulbs caged in yellow
wire. On the floor beneath them were scattered the scraps and
detritus severed from matter in the pursuit of perfection: all
that did not contribute to harmony, luxury, line.

"I'll go, Cosimo. But I want to be late."

He stared, questioning, at the frail girl in front of him.

"I want to be late. Let him wait for me. Let him sit in his

perfect room, alone—repulsive old man—while I make love to you. Here."

"Bethany, *I'm* repulsive."

"Don't ever say that." Crushing against him. "Don't ever say that." Pulling his hand up between her legs so that it finds her. "Cosimo . . ."

Bethany pushed him away and knelt gingerly among the curling scraps of steel. She cleared a space with her hands as Cosimo watched, and lay back on the rough floor in her thin dress.

"You'll be covered in dust."

"Good. Let him see that."

Bethany pulled the dress up to reveal her legs. Cosimo fell awkwardly to his knees, cutting himself.

"Kiss my legs, Cosimo. I'm cold."

He kissed her.

"Between them . . ."

He hesitated.

"That's what I will feel when I dance for the old man. That's what I'm going to think about."

Bethany pulled his head into her, and began to cry. The light, dim but harsh, left almost no shadow. They were naked and hideous beneath the tower.

"I don't know what I'm doing, Cosimo. I don't know what I'm doing. I'm so scared."

He kissed her, as if to banish desiccation. I will drink. And she became liquid. The dust turned to filth on their damp clothes.

When they lifted themselves from the rough floor they were both bruised and coughing; he had a hole in the left knee of his trousers and her dress was ruined. She tossed her underwear

217

away and it fell among the rough pieces scattered about them, the pieces that were not architecture.

Cosimo regarded her with awe. There was some new fierceness burning in her, resigned yet burning: in her passivity she had become rebellious.

"I am ready for him."

I am pleased that we have Tom back with us. Caught between worlds, I have become expert at marking the points of transition. I know when the manhole becomes visible, and on which nights, and I know the times—even more mysterious—when the city's elevators descend beyond their appointed depth, for I am the ferryman, the elevator man, I will take you across the river.

We have crossed the space, the synapse-like abyss where nothing is remembered. We are at the other side. Tom is with us. He will change quickly. Money means very little down here.

The passage into our domain is lethal. By which I mean that it requires the brief erasure of truth. He no longer knows what he once knew. He will learn other things.

Tom moves dazed between the fires. Around them, taking warmth, are gaunt figures. Faces glow red and then duck into shadow, harrowed faces. The poverty is palpable, the men little more than skeletons beneath skin and cloth. It is a community.

Tom turns back to where the elevator stands, barely evident, a prism of quintessence, a theater bounded by air. Something is taking place between these non-walls. He squints in the darkness. Is it possible? In the elevator he has just left, a weeping girl dances.

Cosimo led his friend to the makeshift opening—it was not a door, but a hole in the wall at shoulder height, revealed by a panel of marble removed. It is just large enough to crawl through. A pile of stone blocks—rough stairs—leads up to the opening.

"Come in with me. "

"I can't."

Bethany clutched him, kissed him once with this new strength, equal parts determination and abandon, then turned toward the rough aperture. Cosimo, grieving, left her.

She climbed through the wall. It was dark inside, and for a moment she could see nothing.

"You're late."

I hope to bring all parties together in the end. My brother lives now in Manhattan, my family—what's left of it—in Toronto; I speak to all of them. They will never know that it is me, but I have given them signs, and what I learn down here with my friends informs their lives in oblique ways. Izzy makes theater. He does not know where the images come from; he barely knows the meaning of the words he uses; but I do.

Ariel Price had been standing in the dim light for a long, long time. He could see. When Bethany emerged from the opening, he knew immediately why she had been late: he could see the stains on her dress.

"This is an important occasion—the inauguration of a great

work, the dedication of space. Your invitation was an honor. You are late. You are filthy."

"I am ready."

Ariel Price did not expect this voice. This is not the timid voice he expected.

"You want me to dance for you. Where?"

"In here. This is the center of the Tower. This space stands at the very center. You will be the first and only person to move in this room. Do you understand what an honor this is?"

"And you? You're not a person?"

Ariel's eyes narrowed, but then he smiled. "I am the architect. I stand outside of . . . the ordinary life between these walls."

He began to circle Bethany, making his way slowly toward the opening behind her.

"In fact, I intend to leave this space to you. It is your stage. I do not wish to interfere."

"And you want me to dance?"

"Yes, dance. I shall watch."

The architect climbed through the improvised opening. Bethany watched as he disappeared briefly, then emerged as audience, his head framed by the hole.

She examined the room about her. It was featureless. A box of shining black marble. The only light came from the hole in the wall, obscured mostly by the head of the architect, by the silhouette of his mane. An unsettling sight, her audience. She turned away. Closing her eyes, thinking of her father, Bethany began to dance.

It was less pathetic than her dance in the square. She danced now with an awareness and hatred of her audience. She danced knowing full well that he could see every tear and stain on the back of her dress and that he knew precisely what those signs meant.

Bethany never opened her eyes. She did not have to see the architect to know the despair that she was drawing like blood from his hard arteries. Bethany had learned about men in a dark garage; she knew. Let him watch her.

And because her eyes were closed, Bethany could not see the change that came over the old man's face: how lust gave way to design. Ariel Price was not accustomed to mockery, and he had never failed to emerge triumphant from a contest. Price was an architect: he had fully prepared for this moment.

The shift in illumination would have been barely perceptible, even with her eyes open. The head moving briefly out of its frame to admit a moment's light and then that aperture stopping down, incrementally, brick by brick, as Ariel Price quietly replaced the stone blocks.

It was his finest work. Cosimo had detailed the room, yes, but Ariel had carefully planned the aperture. He had the stone blocks finished so that when properly stacked in their opening the edges met, the tolerance so small that a sheet of paper could not be slid between them. Ariel Price required no mortar. The final block acted as a wedge, locking the pieces together. No merely human force from the interior could dislodge this new wall. Certainly, a young girl would never be able to move one of these stones. God lies in the details.

My studies, careful and professional, over a period of weeks, revealed a remarkable piece of work, perhaps Ariel Price's finest detail: a section of wall designed to fit together like the stones of the Great Pyramid, so perfect in construction and finish that it required no mortar, no fastener, an exercise in pure tectonic virtuosity. The marble panel could be removed without damaging anything—nothing was damaged during the course of my discovery—and the stones could then be dislodged one by one, so long as the proper order was respected and followed. It was like a beautiful puzzle.

Here the fire licked at the serifs and punctuation, but still the final sentence might have been read, had there been any person alive in that room to read it.

And behind that wall—which I carefully dismantled—a perfect room. And within that room, its black marble walls unscarred by the frantic scratching of fingernails, the remarkably well-preserved body of a teenaged girl.

Tom stands rooted and watches in fascination the performance that animates the room in which he has just descended. A young dancer alternating between misery and strength, sometimes breaking the dance to scream silently in pain and claw with exaggerated gestures at the transparent walls.

A hand on his shoulder. He turns. At first he cannot identify her, so meager is the light and her face disfigured with a web of scars, but her voice is unmistakable.

"Hello, Tom."

"Scilla?"

"Let me introduce you to my friends."

He wants to ask her what has been done to her face—the scars look deliberate and precise—but he walks beside her in silence as she takes him from fire to fire.

Huddled about one, reduced to rags but smiling, Tom recognizes three of his secretaries. They lower their eyes, but he knows that they have seen him.

"Do you like the performance?" Scilla's voice is less hard now; she seems truly to care what he thinks of the peculiar dance in the elevator. "I . . . helped with it. I'm doing chore-ography now, Tom.

"You're staring at my face."

Tom averts his eyes, embarrassed.

"It's okay. I cut myself."

"You cut yourself?" Horrified.

"For a long time. Carefully. Like drawing lines. Only I was drawing blood."

"Scilla, that's horrible."

"I didn't feel anything. I don't know why I did it. I'm not sure I ever will. But you know something? Now that I'm living with these people, and helping with the dance, I don't feel any need to cut myself any more."

She smiles. "They're just scars, Tom. You can touch them."

Scilla takes his hand and places it against her skin. Tom is surprised at how good it is to put his hand on her face. The scars are nothing, just lines, raised slightly like ink on Mylar.

"You don't have to stay here, Tom. We—everyone here—we chose exile. You can go back if you want."

Tom says nothing. He continues to touch her face.

"There's not much here. Friendship. We're cut off com-pletely. We have our rituals. Not much."

Tom, reading her face with both hands, makes his decision.

The grand boulevards have become his path of triumph. Ariel Price moves through the streets of Paris, a conquering hero. He has escaped judgment. The biography, ashes now, cannot be discerned from the blood of the biographer, blackened against the floor on rue Esplanade. The architect breathes the fine air of the capital, and marches ecstatic toward his old apartment on Oberkampf. His life purged by refiner's fire, memory conquered, Ariel is reassured in his conviction that the past is merely substance, malleable, awaiting the hand of the architect. My god, this is a beautiful city.

Ariel Price approaches the circus. The cage is there, but it is empty, and he walks by; he does not see the panther pacing, on silent padded feet, the periphery of the faceted cylinder. Odd that they used to design these circuses with the same planimetric conceit as the old panoptical prisons, with the audience captive at the periphery, watched. Ariel moves, the panther circles.

Musing to himself, Ariel reconsiders an early ambition. Could he, the architect, improve upon Paris? It is very well done, Paris. The Vulture had failed. Ariel Price is in an expansive mood, however, and he decides that yes, it would take a great effort of the will, great courage, but he could improve upon this city. In his mind he draws a great X across the urban map, and begins to conceive of a plan. The spaces between the towers! Glorious stretches of park and circulation, the plazas, the plazas . . .

Ice. With a horrible shiver, Ariel Price is made aware of a malevolent gaze. He can feel it, winter, and looking up he identifies the source. A man is staring at him from the doorway of his apartment building. A man almost familiar. Has he met this man before?

Yes, Ariel Price, you have met this man before, although you never properly acknowledged the face, as you never do when transacting with inferiors. For this man is a mere shopkeeper. He has sold you a number of inexpensive products. The man, fatigued after the flight from Montreal, but transcendentally awake now that he has identified with certainty the man who purchased tins of flammable liquid from his *dépanneur*, turns to the gendarme standing behind him in the shadows and hisses, "*C'est lui.*"

And in the ensuing trial, the facts of the life of Ariel Price are placed beneath a forensic microscope, poked and sifted through with patience and rigor, tortured until they reveal nuance unexamined even by the late Theseus Crouch. The cold light of judgment turned to flood every shadow, the darkest spaces lit like fluorescent rooms, described in clinical detail, and fed without pity into a vast eternal transcript.

Arianna cannot sleep. She rarely can. Izzy Darlow makes incoherent noises beside her, deep in another place, his eyes moving behind the lids. She slips out of the bed, still clothed, and stretches. For a moment she examines the sleeping face. Then she walks into the front room.

The walls are hung with pages, the floor still knee-deep in uncut paper. It rustles, a sound like the shifting of rats behind the wall, as Arianna wades through.

She lifts a strand of paper from the floor and begins to read from the center of a paragraph: ". . . standing at the end of the passage. He is framed in dim light, his unnatural posture heightened by the silhouette. This is a man whose spine has been altered; he does not stand as other men stand. He has been changed, structurally; she can see this in an instant. She looks behind her; the long trail of paper is still there. But ahead of her, only this man, in shadow. The paper ends at her feet. He calls out softly.

"Arianna."

She steps forward, leaving for the first time the comforting path. Should she lose sight of the paper unwound behind her, she may never find her way out. She is not sure whether she cares.

"I was hoping you would join us." His voice soothing.

As she approaches, she can make out details of the face. Even in this light, Arianna knows that there is something wrong with this mask, that it too has been altered surgically to hide its origins. But she is not afraid. She holds out her hand. He takes it.

"My name is Jernigan."

"I know."

"I'm glad you're here."

"You're the one I wondered about the most. The one I . . . wanted to meet."

He says nothing, but looks troubled.

"You don't have to tell me anything more about yourself, if you don't want. I like what I read." Arianna touches the tight skin of his face. "You're the one who designed the prison. I like you."

"Does your friend know that you're here?"

"He's asleep. He's not really my friend. I just met him."

Jernigan smiles. "So. Come with me."

Briefly glancing back at the end of the trail of paper, Arianna decides. She will follow this man.

They go a great distance into the gloom of the mall; she no longer knows where she is. Jernigan leads her to the place where he lives.

Arianna examines, her eyes bright with wonder, the mysterious tent of paper and fabric set against the black wall.

"I haven't built much. I designed a . . . room, once, then a prison, and I built this. It may seem strange, but this is the project I'm most proud of. This is my house."

He opens the fabric to reveal the interior space. "My tent in the desert. Will you come inside?"

Arianna smiles. A genuine smile; she feels no hatred toward this man. Without hesitating, she steps inside his home.

Ariel Price is punished with optical precision.

Condemned to spectacle. A saint has her eyes put out, but Ariel Price will see and be seen.

Jernigan Noer, tricked once into designing a windowless prison for an innocent, chooses now to create a prison that is nothing but window. Ariel Price is merged seamlessly with the public space. The man and his work become one.

Arianna turns slowly in the strange interior space, marveling. The walls can be read. It has been put together out of thin stuff, dense with words—notes, torn fabric, pages from books—but the tent is clearly whole, in a way that only something pieced together from fragments can ever be. Arianna walks the periphery, reading.

Jernigan, perched stiffly on an ancient mattress, watches with amusement. "I was hoping you'd come down here to see for yourself."

Arianna smiles over her shoulder. "I knew that you would know how to build a home. Just as I knew that he would not."

"Why did you come to him, then?"

"Not really for shelter. That is how we always announce ourselves. If I'd wanted shelter, I would have turned to you; you clearly know something about sanctuary." She leaves the periphery to sit at Jernigan's feet. "I came for Izzy. To offer him a chance. I know his brother, you see. Josh . . ."

Jernigan nods. They all know Izzy's brother.

"Joshua thought I should go to him, thought I might have . . . something in common." Arianna was silent. She ran her fingers over the tangled half of her mane. "I am also thought to be in rebellion."

"You are."

"Oh yes. I am not happy in my father's house. Not that I matter much; I'm from the lowest order. We can be spared for minor errands. And it doesn't matter much if we are in rebellion."

"And . . . do you have anything in common with Izzy Darlow?"

"Not much. I . . . did not expect him to be so lost. So far removed from the truth. The things that Izzy Darlow doesn't know . . ."

"We're all a bit lost."

"Yes, but what Izzy doesn't know is important. He's obsessed with La Carissima—fine; we all love her—but I know Mary of Magdala. She was never a prostitute. Those men have her completely wrong; they have for centuries; I thought Izzy might prove an exception. Mary's a good person, a sweet person; she always has been. And it wasn't La Carissima had her eyes put out. That was Lucy, Saint Lucy the virgin: she's the one you see standing in those paintings with her eyes in a tray. But men need the Magdalene to be punished. Trust Izzy Darlow to put out a perfectly good woman's eyes."

"He disappointed you."

"Still, I helped him. I helped him with his story. He will still get much wrong, but he knows more than he did before I came."

"I might disappoint you."

"I don't think so."

Arianna leans back, her shoulders against Jernigan's knees. He places a hand on the back of her neck. She does not move. The hand on her neck trembles. She stills it with her own. "I know who you are. I can see through lies. I don't tell lies, so they don't work on me. I know what they did to your body to hide the truth. I could see it right away. The operations, what they did. They straightened your back, didn't they."

Cosimo squeezes her shoulder, desperately: stop. She says nothing more.

Arianna stands gracefully and faces the man. They find each other's eyes. Hers strong, unwavering; his terrified behind the mask. She pulls her nightdress over her head in an easy movement and remains in front of him, unashamed, her legs slightly apart but turned inward, one hand on her neck. Cosimo can no longer meet her eyes.

In a space removed from this by something less tangible than physical distance, Izzy Darlow sleeps.

Arianna takes Cosimo's hand gently and places it against her thin breast. The hand is still shaking. The skin beneath the frightened fingers tight and cold. She moves forward, awkward now, putting her breast against his lips. He opens his mouth. Arianna closes her eyes; they feel vulnerable to steel. Guiding his hand carefully, indicating her need with the urgency of her fingers, she introduces it to the white place on the inside of her thigh. Cosimo moves his hand to cradle her; his hand is wet. "Why are you doing this?"

"Because I know who you are. I know how kind you were to that girl, Bethany." She sucks in her breath sharply as his fingers swim into her. "I . . . like that I'm down here with you, and that he's somewhere else, sleeping, dreaming of how he's going to seduce me when he wakes up. Yes, touch me there."

The walls, although no one reads them now, tell a layered story. Despite the woman shuddering, barely able to stand in the center of the tent as her legs are made to shiver, the walls tell their story in measured sentences: the text moves only as quickly as it was written. Some of the passages older than others, written in an adolescent hand. The boy with the gash on his forehead, Arianna's friend, wrote these when he was alive and young. He has collected them in his visits to the ruins of that house; he has combined them with notes made after the fire, with passages written by others whose words began to bleed into his. Here is a page from the preface to the biography of Ariel Price; here is a torn corner of vellum with notes in the architect's hand. Here, in the tent which is a book, Arianna presses her thin body against the flushed skin of the architect's assistant. The words, collected against the wind that would disperse them, have been woven into shelter. Sanctuary. Death and the architect elsewhere.

Ariel Price, white with horror, stands at the threshold of his cell and looks into his punishment. A wall of words. Not fixed but falling: a cascade of words, scrolling, lit red, falling eternally into the stone floor. A transcript.

As he reads the scrolling text—and it is clear that he is not alone, that spectators come to watch his torment are reading these words as well—Ariel begins to comprehend the true weight of his sentence. For there, in bright eternal text, falling past his cell (which is little more than an optical device, a scope, a window) is the complete and unedited *Life of Price*. The book of him.

If damnation is distance, then the extent of Ariel's fall can be measured precisely: it is the span from his cornea to that wall of text, the distance of reading, the unnavigable space—the inverse of Lethe—across which memory is preserved, incapable of destruction. Frozen with shame, our modern Prometheus stands chained in his cell, and history visits relentlessly and without pity, eating away at the organs of his soul.

Stein Foregutt basks in the light reflected from his latest masterpiece, explaining in sesquipedalian terms the ineluctable forces of history and theory that required that he, Stein Foregutt, should become the instrument of the great man's punishment. And Jernigan Noer, after explaining to Foregutt the meaning of the work to which the famous man has signed his name, disappears.

On an unremarkable evening, a young prostitute is beaten to death by a group of teenage boys, and the body is left to freeze in the circling wind of the Letztesmann Plaza. Clutched in Sarah's hand is a rock of ordinary salt.

Izzy Darlow awakens with a woman breathing softly against his arm. Arianna, dressed now, lies stretched out beside him. Her closed eyes move in the pace of a dream. Her face untroubled. Days of hatred, nights of recrimination, built tyranny: this moment, the narrator decides, is sufficient to redeem.

The sea of paper twisting on his floor and nailed in pieces to his wall has dried to bone. Today he will cut the rest of the scroll into pages; he will take this miraculous yield into the empty theater. And when the actors gather round, he will spread the paper on the stage. Izzy Darlow rehearses in his mind what he will say to them: I don't know what we have here. I don't know what it is. But I believe we have a text.

Tomorrow Arianna will leave him and never return. But he does not know this. Her breath human against his arm.